CESTUS

BY ARLEY VEST

Copyright © 2013 Arley Vest
All rights reserved.
ISBN: 098931460X
ISBN 13: 9780989314602
Library of Congress Control Number: 2013908709
Lazarus Literary Cartersville, GA

Be it known therefore unto you, that the salvation of God is sent unto the Gentiles, and that they will hear it.
Acts 28:28

I

What were the stars? he wondered. Why did they only appear at night? And the moon? Was it a great rock in the sky? A jewel placed there by the gods? Whatever it was, it must be very far away. He had tried to reach it with arrows, but no matter how far back he pulled the bowstring, he didn't come close.

From his sleeping place outside his parents' hut, the youth regarded the heavens in solitary awe. The night air was cold about his shoulders, but he closed his mind to the discomfort. As the eldest son of the leader of the clan, it was fitting that he learn to sleep apart and harden himself. Besides, he was old enough at fourteen summers to know of his father and mother's need for privacy, and old enough to seek privacy himself.

Pale wisps of smoke hung in the blue-black stillness of the dawning light—thin ghosts of campfires that had perished with the night. From a nearby meadow came the first delicate echo of birdsongs. At the edge of the camp a dog barked once, twice, and then was silent.

It was the last sleep before a new day, but the boy had been awake for some time, engrossed in great mysteries. The moon was low to the ground now. It moved through the sky—and it changed in size and shape. Sometimes it was round and full, and at other times it was smaller and part of it was missing. He had asked about such things, but no one could explain them, not even his father.

The tip of the sun would appear over the ridge soon, another mystery. The youth wrapped his blanket about his shoulders and quietly made his way to the lookout hill. It was good to see the day come to life from a high place, and good as well to be in the company of the sentry. One day soon he would be old enough to stand watch, and he must learn how to conduct himself.

As he started up the incline, he heard something tumbling down toward him. He halted, searching quickly through the gray half-light, confident of his ability to dodge a falling rock, yet aware that the sound (a slow dull thumping roll, strangely low and muted) was too soft for a stone. Suddenly it was upon him, and he stood rooted in open-mouthed horror as the thing much softer than a stone—the severed and bloody head of the sentry—bounced one final time and came to rest against his foot.

A soundless cry stuck in his throat. Gagging, unable to either draw air in or force it out, he jerked his foot away in a furious spasm that sent the blanket to the ground but failed to dislodge the grisly head.

For several seconds he stood there, struggling against a sudden warm rush of nausea, then he heard a rumbling sound as of thunder. Looking up, he saw dark shapes of horsemen plunging from the sky.

He found his voice, and with it his legs. Shouting out an alarm, he went racing for his father's tent, but the thunder of hooves overtook him before he reached the embers of the first campfire.

When he awoke, he thought he was in the afterworld. All about him was a thick, dark haze through which tongues of fire spit and crackled. Then he felt a thudding pain in his head and knew that he was still in the land of the living. He sat halfway up, searching through smoke and confusion for his family. Before he could get to his feet, rough hands grabbed him and tied his wrists with rope. Frightened and bewildered and reeling with shock, the sickening odor of mutilated flesh mingling with ashes in his throat, he saw that others were alive, but his father and mother and sister were not among them.

The survivors who looked to be of value were rounded up, twelve in all, seven women and girls and five men and boys. The males were linked to one long rope, and the females to another, and the lines made fast. The youth of fourteen and a girl named Elena found themselves close to one another. He saw the fear in her eyes, but also the resolute set of her mouth in this most terrible of times, and his heart went out to her.

"Elena..." he whispered.

"Steppan..." she whispered in return.

The crack of a whip silenced them both.

All that day the captives were prodded along, moving southward, away from the mountains and toward the land of the Romans. When at last they halted for the night, even the most hopeful among them lay down with the awful knowledge that they were destined to be sold for coins.

At dawn they were given water and cakes of wheat, then herded along again, shuffling and limping and stumbling until the day began to burn down toward darkness. Another sparse meal, and then they were committed to the ground for a few hours of fitful rest.

Late afternoon of the third day, they halted on the bank of a river. The captives were fed, then the females were sent under guard to bathe, for they were nearing their destination.

The women and girls closed their eyes to the shame of being watched as they shed their ragged clothing. Huddling together, they slipped into the water, lowering themselves down as far as they could. The leader of the slavers, a burly black-bearded man who wore a rawhide whip coiled about his shoulder much as other men wore a shirt, remained with the bath detail for a while, leering and making jokes with his men, then turned back toward camp.

As soon as black-beard was safely out of sight, one of the guards went to the water's edge and beckoned the girl named Elena out of the stream. She looked beseechingly about, nearly paralyzed with fear, but the other females avoided her eyes, hoping their captors would be content with her alone.

The guard motioned impatiently and called to her again. And when she began to back away, he waded in after her, brandishing a knife to ensure her submission. "Now then…" he panted, smirking to his comrades as he hauled the naked and trembling girl out to the riverbank "…give me a while with her, then come and have your turn." Without waiting for an answer, he dragged Elena through some bushes and pushed her to the ground.

A fetid odor of dirt and animal skins closed about her, a mouth filled with foul breath pressed hard against her lips, and hands thick and clumsy explored her body. For unmeasured moments she laid there, the blood pounding thickly in her head. Then he touched her where no man ever had, and a desperate fury pushed her fear aside. He leaned back to unfasten his belt, and suddenly a barbarian wildcat was upon him, scratching and gouging and kicking. A sharp knee found his groin and he let out a strangled moan and rolled over on his side.

As the would-be attacker groveled about in search of his breath, the leader of the slavers came crashing through the bushes. "Idiot!" he bellowed. "I gave orders not to touch the women! I ought to wrap this…!" he uncoiled the whip and brandished it aloft, but then his roar of anger gave way to laughter. "Ho! It looks like I came just in time to rescue you!" He let loose another laugh, and then turned his attention to the girl.

"Well, now," he grunted, looking Elena over appraisingly. "She is a juicy little piece! But if we have our way with her, we'll ruin the goods. And with the price she'll bring, we could all buy a whore for a week. So I say let her go…" Having so spoken, he allowed his man to save face by appearing to let the question hang in the air.

The chastened guard nodded his assent, not trusting his voice to give an answer.

"Good! Now go help fetch the others out of the water and bring them back to camp. Meanwhile, I'll put this one back in to wash off the dust." He nudged Elena with the whip, pushing her out of the clearing and back into the stream, all the while measuring her with quick, furtive glances. He waited until the guards and their freshly washed captives were on their way, then picked up Elena's clothing and waved it aloft.

Trying to cover herself with her hands, she came out of the water for the second time, casting her eyes anywhere but upon his. He would do her no harm, she thought desperately. After all, it was he who had rescued her from the other; he who had said she must be kept pure. But when she reached out for her clothing, he snatched it away and grabbed her.

"Listen!" he hissed, his voice harsh and rasping. "It's either me or all of them! Understand? Me or all of them," he repeated, using the coiled up whip to caress her breasts. Satisfied that she would obey his commands, he shoved her back into the same clearing from which she had been delivered.

By the time the males were brought to bathe, the sun was lowering, so they were hurried roughly along. But the boy Steppan was oblivious to kicks and shoves and curses. He knew that when he reached the land of the Romans, his life would be an endless round of humiliation and torment and pain. But he also knew that he was not without a final choice. He could take the life they thought they owned—and rob them of their bloody profit as well. So when he stepped into the stream with the others, he did not stay in the shallows but waded further and further out until his was near the middle, where the current was swift and deep.

The guards went running to the edge of the riverbank, shouting for him to stop, but Steppan kept on until he disappeared beneath the surface. Wondering fleetingly if he would meet his family in the hereafter, he willed himself to take a breath, to let the water flow into his lungs. He forced his lips apart, felt the heavy, brackish rush…then shot up choking and gasping for air.

No!

He would not let them bring him to a coward's death.

He would survive!

Somehow, he would survive.

II

"Marcellus! Wake up!" Lucius Cornelius Portius shook his son by the shoulder, frowning impatiently as covers slowly stirred, a head tentatively poked forth, and eyes gradually registered signs of life.

"Come now! Up! Up, or we shall be too late!" Portius barked. Then he spun about and went striding out of the bedchamber, shaking his head in frustration. He was one of the wealthiest and most powerful men in all of Rome, but as far as his son was concerned, he might as well be a peasant on a farm. How could it be that he commanded such great respect from others and so little from his own flesh and blood? Especially since that flesh and blood not only thoroughly enjoyed but stood to inherit the fruits of all that the father had accomplished, all that the Portius name had come to embody.

Though he was an aristocrat by birth, Lucius Cornelius Portius had not been content to rest on that fact. As a younger man, he had painstakingly crafted a glittering military reputation. At the height of his career, he led campaigns into Cisalpine Gaul, Spain, and the northern tip of Africa, all of which earned him not only the expressed gratitude of the senate and acclaim from the citizenry of Rome, but a considerable increase in his personal fortune as well. Somehow, not all of the tribute extracted by conquest found its way to the Imperial Treasury.

From celebrated military hero (albeit one who was an officer, not a warrior) to the senate was but a natural progression for a man possessed of both eminent family status and burning ambition. Once seated in that august body, Portius prospered all the more. In time his business holdings expanded to include interests ranging from mining (silver in Spain and iron in North Africa) to ranching (a vast cattle ranch in Epirus) to real estate (tracts of farmland plus numerous tenements) to banking. And, of course, there was the family estate and the family treasury.

His countryside villa at Alba Longa offered eloquent testimony to his prosperity. Situated among some two hundred elegantly landscaped acres, the main house was built of marble and stone and contained three dining rooms, a banquet hall, a kitchen capable of servicing all three dining areas at once, twelve bedchambers, an art room, a library, a parlor, a private study, a lararium for the household gods, and several rooms for bathing.

There were also extensive servant's quarters, and, most important to the master of the estate, there were the stables. Considerable attention had been lavished on the stables and the accompanying exercise area and racetrack, for not only were his horses a source of great pride to their owner, they also brought him a healthy income from racing matches.

Quite naturally, such an estate required a proper number of slaves. At latest count there were nearly a hundred, yet Lucius Portius's wife considered the villa to be understaffed. She was particularly concerned that the slave woman who had long been in charge of Lady Claudia's garments had recently died without so much as giving proper notice, thereby leaving a serious void.

And thus it was that Lucius Portius, having grown weary of Claudia's complaints, had made plans to set out that very day to personally remedy the situation. And Marcellus Servianus was to accompany him.

If, that is, the boy could ever manage to rouse himself from the comfort of his bed.

When at last Portius and his son departed, only one manservant accompanied them, a trusted driver and bodyguard. Despite the presence of the driver, Portius handled the reins of the chariot himself, hoping to impress his son with his prowess and instruct him at the same time. There were, in fact, several things he wished to show young Marcellus Servianus this day. For one, Marcellus had not yet visited any of the slave markets. It was time, the elder Portius thought, for the boy to get out of the house and see what was going on in the rest of the world.

What the boy saw on his first glimpse of the world of the slave market was a dusty, crowded, noisy place reeking with offensive odors. His father, however, seemed almost to revel in it all, steering through the noise and confusion with an air of accustomed ease. When they came to a broad raised platform near the center of the market, the senior Portius halted and called out to a heavy-set man in an ill-fitting tunic.

"Rufus!"

The one named Rufus looked about, discovered the source of the voice, and came hurrying toward it. "It is good to see you, General," he said in greeting, using the form of address he knew the other man favored even above the title of senator.

As Rufus drew near, Marcellus Servianus's delicate nostrils were assailed by yet another unpleasant odor. Perhaps it was the tunic, Marcellus thought, noting that the garment was badly soiled. He also noticed that, though the man was carrying an unfortunate measure of fat over a frame that held considerable muscle, he was not altogether bad looking. He had a full head of dark hair and pleasantly rugged features. But the smell!

"Well, what have you to show today?" Lucius Portius asked, getting right down to business.

"Ah…some splendid Nubians," Rufus began. "Tall men, strongly formed. And a few equally well-formed women. One or two actually quite choice, if you get my meaning…"

Portius shook his head. "I have had some unfortunate experiences with Nubians. What else do you have?"

"A number of commendable Greeks," Rufus replied hopefully. "Several of them quite well educated."

"Any females trained in the art of the wardrobe?"

"Unfortunately not. However, there are one or two males—sensitive types—who, with the right training, would be well-suited in that capacity."

"No. No males for that task. What else?"

"Well…a few barbarians. Mostly women and children. But very sturdy. I assure you, it would be well worth your time to at least stay and view them."

"Yes," Portius agreed. "Stay I will. If not precisely to view your wares, then at least to acquaint this young man with the devious practices of the marketplace."

"Ah, then this must be your son!" Rufus exclaimed, mentally chastising himself for not having acknowledged the presence of the youth standing there with wrinkled and upturned nose. "A fine-looking young man. Would he be your eldest?"

"My only son. Marcellus Servianus."

Rufus made a bow in the direction of the youngster. "Hail, Marcellus Servianus."

Marcellus Servianus sniffed and nodded briefly.

A soft, pale-looking little slug, Rufus thought. No doubt his hands had never known so much as a single day's work. There was nothing in any aspect of his physical appearance to suggest he had sprung from the loins of the elder Portius. But he was an arrogant little piece of shit—a perfect copy of the father in that respect.

"Well," Rufus said, straightening up, "I must see about getting the auction underway. If I can be of any service…" He bowed again, and turned to attend to his duties.

The sale progressed much as Lucius Portius expected. The Nubians were far from splendid. Most of them, even the women, were lacking in weight to the point of being gaunt. No doubt they had suffered from captivity, he thought, but they were still an inferior lot.

The Greeks, except for two who sold right off, were not much better. Portius was by then bored with the proceedings, but, inasmuch as Claudia had been so persistently vocal in expressing her dire need, he stayed awhile longer.

The barbarians were the last to be brought forth. They, too, were disappointing as a whole—the women generally too old and the children too young for his needs. But there was one girl of promise. She appeared to be in her late teens—a large girl but shapely, fair of hair and skin, and not at all unattractive. Perhaps, Portius thought, he could obtain a double bargain.

He ordered her brought closer and turned before him, asked questions, bargained more briefly than was his custom, and sealed the price.

His main purpose accomplished, Portius made ready to leave, but the words of the slave exhibitor halted him.

"…still only a youth, yet note how tall and well formed he is. And he is already most skilled in the handling of horses…"

Skilled in the handling of horses!

Turning his attention back to the platform, Portius studied the youth. Large, indeed, for one so apparently young. Broad shouldered, well muscled, already more man than boy. Somewhat darker of hair and skin than most of his group, no doubt of mixed blood. The gods only knew what strange mixtures flowed through the veins of barbarians!

As he examined the boy, Portius began to formulate a solution to a situation that had become increasingly vexing. Marcellus Servianus was sorely lacking in horsemanship. Indeed, he showed a distinct disinterest toward any of the arts of war. Yet it was vital that the young man lay the proper foundation for success that had been carefully plotted: build first the discipline of the body that leads to discipline of the mind, utilize such training to forge a solid military career, then proceed in measured and logical steps into the uppermost reaches of the twin worlds of business and politics, carrying the Portius name to ever greater heights, ever greater glory.

Unfortunately, the first step had not even been embarked upon; all efforts at instruction in any sort of physical skill had been met with persistent indifference. Perhaps, however, with a tutor nearer Marcellus's own age, someone he might feel more comfortable with than the older veterans of battle he had heretofore been entrusted to...

Still, there was something about this young barbarian that gave pause. At first glance there was the expected presence of fear that even the hardest of men, let alone boys, found difficult to mask when they were stripped and brought to market. A second, closer look uncovered something else with this one, however. Portius almost dismissed it as pride; but then he recognized what that pride had been translated into: a fierceness, a smoldering fury that a less observant man might not have noticed because it was a controlled fury...the worst kind.

Shrugging off his misgivings, for it was only a youth and could easily be trained, he put up a finger to signal a bid.

III

The crowd had been gathering along the banks of the River Jordan since early that morning. Many of the people had come from some distance away, most of them on foot. A few of the more fortunate rode donkeys, and fewer still—those seriously ill or infirm—were carried on litters. As the sun mounted in the sky, the crowd swelled greatly, and at length a grumbling arose among the people. Where was he? some of them began to demand. Perhaps he was not coming. Perhaps they had all gathered there for nothing.

Voices became louder and louder, the cries of small children more persistent, the moans and pleas of the suffering increasingly pitiful. Some made ready to leave, for the sun was strong and there was little food or drinkable water to be found nearby.

Suddenly, one voice rang out above the others.

"There he is!"

Heads turned, fingers pointed, eyes went eagerly seeking.

The one they had all been awaiting, the man named Zebediah, called by many a prophet, a true man of God, approached from upstream, accompanied by a small band of followers. Though of medium height, he was so lean that he seemed taller, and the flowing whiteness of his hair and beard were in such stark contrast to the sunbaked darkness of his skin that eyes were pulled to him like iron to a lodestone.

As he drew nearer, a hush fell over the crowd. Then suddenly the people surged forward with an even greater clamor than before, each one wanting to see, to hear, to touch…to be the first.

Staff in hand, he strode resolutely forward, his disciples clearing a path through the throng until they reached the summit of a gently sloping hill. There Zebediah paused and closed his eyes in prayer, leaning on his staff for support.

For several moments he stood silent and unmoving, and then he opened his eyes and turned toward the assemblage. As he did so, his disciples moved up closer and sat down about him, and the multitude began to recline as well.

Zebediah waited yet awhile longer, letting the crowd quiet down. Just before he spoke, he did something seemingly uncharacteristic of a prophet. He smiled.

The smile reflected itself among the masses, spreading from face to face, breaking down the many barriers of pain and fear and doubt and suffering. Many believed that Zebediah had the true gift of prophecy, that the things he spoke were revelations from God. And others said that he had the power to heal and do other miraculous deeds. Thus, when he smiled, the people took it as a good omen and opened themselves to his words.

When the words came, they were not formed of thunder and lightning, as those who had not heard him speak before might have expected, but of peace and joy and love.

"Rejoice," he told his listeners, "for God's love dwells within you. Many among you know suffering," he said. "Many among you are downtrodden and weary. But rejoice, then, all the more, for even as a loving parent disciplines a favorite child so that the child might learn and thus prosper later in life, so our loving Father chastises us in order that we might learn and thus come to know his glory.

"Therefore accept what has been allotted to you without envying others," he enjoined. "For no one knows what lives within the heart of another, or what the new day might bring. Neither should you concern yourself with the ways of those who seek dominion in this world, for the things of this earth soon pass away, as do all those who walk upon it.

"Such things are difficult for us to see," he admitted. "Yet what man could count the drops of rain that fall upon the earth? Or account for the stars that appear in the sky? Neither can a man comprehend the wisdom of the Almighty. Yet there are signs to point the way."

What Zebediah said next was as startling to many in the crowd as any unleashing of thunder or lightning. "The Lord gives us guidance by speaking to us," he declared. "Not merely to a chosen few, such as the prophets of old, but to every living person, man, woman, and child, rich and poor alike. We have but to listen," he said. "Listen to the voice within.

"The voice of the world," he expounded, "says, 'Set the price at five coins, for this man is fool enough to pay.' But the voice within replies, 'No, three is fair enough. Any more would be robbery.'

"And again, the voice of the world proclaims, 'My neighbor has offended me. I will take up my sword against him.' But the voice within cautions, saying, 'Hold! He is but a man, even as yourself. Seek, then, to forgive him so that when you in turn offend, you might be forgiven.'"

Zebediah paused for a moment, his head cocked to one side as if listening to a voice no one else could hear. Then he resumed speaking, but now his words were more hurried.

"But I have not been sent to you this day only to speak such words, for you have heard them before, and from far better tongues than mine. No, this day I have been sent with a message of great joy. For long has a savior been promised, and now the promise has been fulfilled."

At these words a great wave of excitement ran through the crowd. Those near the back pressed forward, straining to hear, and for the first time since Zebediah had begun to speak voices were raised.

"You say the savior has already been sent among us?" one man called out. "Who is he, then? And where can we find him?"

"When his time is come, he will be made known," Zebediah answered.

"But how will we recognize him?" another demanded, a question echoed by others.

"And how is it," the first questioner persisted, "that none of us know of this savior if he already lives? Surely he must be a great warrior if he is to deliver us from our oppressors. Tell us where we might find him, so that we might join his forces."

Zebediah shook his head. "The Messiah will not come carrying the sword of death, but rather holding forth the staff of life."

As these last words were uttered, a man at the rear of the throng turned toward a low rise of hills behind him and raised his arm in a signal. Almost instantly a column of horsemen, the riders clad in the dreaded armor of Roman cavalry, appeared on the horizon.

One of Zebediah's followers caught a glimpse of sunlight on metal and sounded a cry of alarm. For most, the warning came too late. Unarmed and unsuspecting, their ranks dotted with women and children and the aged and infirm, the gathering was an easy prey for the Romans.

What transpired was not what had been ordered, however. The soldiers had merely been instructed to locate and disperse the assembly and arrest the leaders. For while men such as Zebediah were looked on by the local emissaries of

Rome as rabble-rousing troublemakers, they were not considered truly dangerous. As it happened, however, when the cavalry came charging down the hill, followed by several maniples of foot soldiers, a hot-headed young Judean thrust his dagger into the thigh of the wing commander.

Though the wound was superficial, the act so horrified the officer, a young patrician named Justinian Flavius, that he began swinging his sword in utter panic, all the while shouting out a series of totally incomprehensible commands. In short order Flavius cut down an unarmed youth barely more than a boy, ran his sword through a cripple afflicted with cataracts, and trampled beneath his horse a woman intent on nothing more menacing than attempting to flee.

Inspired by his example, his troops vented their own fears and angers and frustrations with such mindless abandon that the operation quickly degenerated into a massacre. In less than the fourth part of an hour, the awful operation was completed. Bodies lay maimed and lifeless along the slope, trails of blood stained the dark surface of the river, and from the low valley there arose a broken wail of lamentation.

Incredibly enough, Zebediah was among those few who managed to escape. Later some claimed that he had joined hands with his closest followers and walked across the surface of the Jordan and into the wilderness beyond. The truth was far less miraculous but effective nonetheless. As Justinian Flavius was stirring his troops into a frenzy, a sturdy young man named Jarel, a distant relative of Zebediah and one of his most steadfast disciples, took the prophet by the arm and led him away from the river, where the Romans were occupied with their deadly work, and up the hill and across the valley.

In the weeks that followed, word of Zebediah's deliverance blossomed into something of a legend. From town to town and village to village, in the hills and valleys from lower Judea to upper Galilee, the story was told countless times and seldom the same way twice.

Zebediah had made his escape by walking on water as if it were firmament.

The hills had opened to receive him and closed again after his passing, much like the Red Sea had parted for Moses.

The Romans had somehow been struck blind to the prophet's presence; they could see other people but not him.

Regardless of the exact circumstances of his escape, it was generally agreed that some sort of miracle had occurred. And in light of such an event, Zebediah must indeed be considered a man chosen by the Lord, a man such as the prophets of old.

On the Roman side of the fence, it was quite a different story. The official word passed along to Rome was that a detachment of troops led by Captain Justinian Flavius had encountered a large group of seditious Jews near the city of Jericho. Inasmuch as the Jews put up a determined resistance, they had to be routed with all necessary force. There was not, however, a single casualty on the Roman side.

Because of the condition of some of the bodies, it had not been possible to determine if the leader of the zealots, a man named Zebediah, was among the slain. Neither had he been counted among those taken prisoner. Nonetheless, the dispatch continued, even if he had somehow managed to flee, there was little likelihood that he would ever resume his activities again.

As a result of the action by the river, Captain Justinian Flavius was given an official commendation.

IV

Lucius Portius had both of his new slaves delivered to the villa at Alba Longa. The girl was sent to the main house, the boy to the equestrian area where he was turned over to Quatro, a slave of long tenure and the one in charge of the equestrian area.

Quatro was a man of indeterminate age. The leathery skin of his face and shaved head was in such contrast to the chiseled muscularity of his physique that it seemed as if the heads and bodies of two different men had been transposed. Speaking slowly and with broad gestures of his hands, for he had been told the youth knew nothing of Greek and little of Latin, he gave Steppan a brief tour of the place where he would labor. The equestrian area was open and expansive, but only when he came to the shadowed and musty stables did Steppan's eyes betray any interest.

The change, though subtle, did not go unnoticed.

"Do you like horses?" Quatro asked, nodding toward the animals milling about in their stalls.

By way of answer, Steppan went over and ran his hand softly along the neck and mane of one of the creatures.

From the stables they went to the unadorned wooden structure barracks where the equestrian workers were quartered. It contained a common room for eating, a number of tiny cells for sleeping, and what appeared to be a very small stone pond, halfway submerged in the middle of a room at the rear of the barracks.

"That is where you will bathe," Quatro told him, a statement that brought only a puzzled look. "You will be given food and clothing. In the morning I will come to show you your duties. Until then, rest." Quatro walked a few paces away, and then turned. "It will be all right," he said quietly. "You could have been sent to far worse places."

Steppan was sitting up waiting when Quatro returned shortly after dawn. In the beginning he was kept busy cleaning the stables and feeding horses. After the first month, one hour every other day was set aside for tutoring in Latin and Greek. A slave of the family of Lucius Portius had to be able to comprehend basic commands in either language, and so Steppan was turned over to the Greek who was librarian and tutor.

Before the first language lesson, as with each successive one, Steppan was ordered to bathe. Once Steppan was clean, Quatro led him to the main house of the estate to meet his tutor. Steppan's slow-paced wonder at the unfolding landscape of formal gardens with meticulously tended trees and shrubs and marble statues of gods and goddesses made the normally ten-minute walk much longer. Occasionally Steppan would come to a halt and tentatively reach out to touch one of the mythical stone creatures.

The grandeur of the gardens paled, however, in comparison to the sight of the sprawling stone mansion. Were Quatro not with him, Steppan would not have dared enter such a magnificent structure. As it was, Quatro led him to an antechamber that led to yet another garden, told his young charge that he would return within an hour, and disappeared.

During that hour, Steppan discovered yet another amazing thing. The Greek, a short man with small, soft hands, could look at markings on a piece of thin cloth and translate those marks into words. Equally amazing, he could do the reverse, take words that were spoken and make the marks that signified their meaning.

Could he, Steppan inquired, learn to do this magical thing himself? Along with learning the two new tongues, of course.

Pleased that someone had been sent to him who actually wanted to learn (and not at all displeased that this new slave boy was quite handsome as well), the tutor smilingly agreed.

As the weeks went by, the new slave boy was given the additional tasks of helping to groom the horses and lead them to and from the exercise area. It was readily apparent that the boy was a good worker, steady and strong and willing. Moreover, he had a way with horses. He was at ease with them, firm and unafraid, yet gentle. Soon he would be ready to exercise the animals, and then he would be tested as a rider and trainer.

He would, Quatro was certain, do very well.

If he did not die first.

In the time Steppan had been at Alba Longa he had lost a noticeable amount of weight. Instead of relaxing somewhat as he became more familiar with his surroundings, he seemed to grow more nervous and despondent. At mealtimes he picked at his food. And when Quatro looked in on him at night, more often than not, the youth was awake.

Finally, Quatro took him aside.

"Do you want to live?" he asked bluntly.

Startled, Steppan looked at the older man for a few moments before nodding affirmatively.

"Good. But wanting to live is not enough. You must will it. When food is offered, eat. When night comes and you are given rest, take it. To survive, you must be strong. Strong in body and in mind."

Steppan shook his head uncertainly. "I want to live, but it is so hard, being…not free."

"Yes, it is hard to be a slave," Quatro said, pronouncing the word with deliberate emphasis to show that it could be uttered. "So you must strengthen yourself. Tonight I will bring you something to help you sleep. Once you have slept, you will eat. When you eat, you will grow strong. And when you are strong, you can survive."

That night Quatro brought Steppan a cup containing a mixture of wine and herbs and stayed until the boy drained it.

"Remember," Quatro counseled in parting, "to survive, you must be strong."

The potion acted swiftly and powerfully. The numbness started in his toes then spread to his legs and along his trunk to his neck and face and at last to his brain, where finally it transported him into the temporary relief of unbroken slumber.

Marcellus Servianus Portius grew up with slaves. That is, they attended to him from the day of his birth. Because of his father's wealth, Marcellus's food, drink, clothing, shelter, comfort, education, and even amusement were looked after by a progression of silent, anonymous beings.

Even so, or perhaps because it was so, he gave the matter of slaves and slavery very little thought. A slave was simply meant to be a slave. They were, regardless of origin, a race apart, creatures in some measure less than human. Instruments without a voice, was the common expression. Not "he" or "she" but "it." Thus, when a new slave boy appeared at Alba Longa, it was some time before Marcellus Servianus even noticed that another "it" had been added to the landscape.

He soon enough discovered, however, that this new one was different. This slave had been procured especially for him, but not to serve him at mealtimes or look after his wardrobe. No, this one—who was not much more than a boy himself—was to instruct him! It was, young Marcellus immediately decided, a simply intolerable notion.

On the occasion of his first scheduled lesson in horsemanship, Marcellus Servianus haughtily informed Quatro that he would not mount a horse that day. Rather, he declared, he would learn by watching.

Quatro bowed silently and retreated to the track to watch Steppan put a stallion through its paces, noting the improvement in the boy's health. After Quatro spoke to him, Steppan had remained quiet and withdrawn, but he ate everything put on his plate. On some mornings he even had to be awakened. And since beginning arduous drills in the combat arts, skills that he would in turn be required to attempt to transmit to his owner's son, Steppan's youthful frame had filled out with impressive adult-sized muscles.

Young Marcellus Servianus remained in the shaded comfort of the grandstand for only a short while, looking on with studied boredom before making his way back to the comfort of the villa. He thought that the next time he visited the stable area, if there were a next time, he'd make the trip by litter rather than on foot.

It turned out that Marcellus badly underestimated the extent of the elder Portius's determination. When the family gathered for the evening meal, the father issued a stern and explicit command.

The next morning Marcellus Servianus appeared again at the stables, on foot, and stated that he had reconsidered and was now ready to actively take part in the learning process.

So the task began, and if Marcellus Servianus did not relish this part of his education, neither did Steppan. In all truth, the slave boy much preferred to work with horses. Nonetheless, Lucius Portius's intuition about a more youthful instructor proved to be essentially correct, even if not for the exact reasons he had supposed.

Perhaps it was because Marcellus Servianus decided to show his father that he could, if he so desired, measure up. Perhaps it was because Marcellus did, indeed, feel more confident with someone not only nearer his age but also a slave, not a soldier. Or perhaps it had to do with Steppan's attitude. He was as patient as any slave had to be, but he was also more direct than the veterans who had preceded him. Whether or not the Roman boy learned was, to his mind, really up to the Roman boy. Whatever the reason or combination of reasons, the Roman boy actually showed signs of progress. In a relatively short time, the young Portius overcame enough of his fear of the great four-legged beasts to mount and ride with at least a passable semblance of competence.

Informed by Quatro of his son's growing skills, Lucius Portius came to observe. As he watched Marcellus bring his horse past the grandstand, he congratulated himself on having chosen the slave boy as tutor. Not only was Marcellus almost at ease on a horse, he was also looking more fit.

When his eyes lingered in turn on his son's tutor, however, he could not help but note that the slave boy was not only surpassingly more skilled, but far more muscular as well. Moreover, he seemed to possess a confidence that totally belied his station. A natural-born warrior, Portius mused. He had campaigned against tribes of such men, fierce unrelenting fighters, and the sight of the youth joined so naturally with the horse brought an involuntary shudder of remembrance. Barbarians! More than one general of the Roman army was of the opinion that though the barbarians might be overwhelmed in battle, they were never quite conquered.

Turning, Lucius Portius shrugged away such thoughts and headed back to the villa. The other new slave, the girl Elena, was a different type of barbarian. Quite a lovely thing, once she had been properly cleaned up. Fair-skinned, full-figured, ripe with promise. And fearful enough so that while her eyes objected and her body stiffened unbecomingly, she made no sound or movement of protest when he caressed her. Soon, he thought, smiling broadly to himself, he would really and truly make her his slave. Soon he would conquer that little barbarian. Conquer her fully.

V

Because Lady Claudia did not share her husband's enthusiasm for horses, she seldom ventured down to the stables at Alba Longa. The only time she found any enjoyment in the equestrian area was during races, for then there was an air of festivity with wine, laughter, an interesting array of guests, and a certain element of both drama and danger that was at least a distant cousin to the Games. In all truth, now that the newness of Alba Longa had worn off, she had less and less desire to visit the place at all. It was, of course, magnificent, for she had actively immersed herself in the details of decoration and design, but it was so...remote. So far removed from the excitement and convenience of the city.

Unfortunately for Claudia, as her enthusiasm for the country estate dwindled, that of her husband escalated. For Lucius Portius, Alba Longa had become a sanctuary from the hectic, backstabbing world of politics and money and power. Even more, it was a place where he truly was emperor of all he surveyed, and so his visits there became not only more frequent but more prolonged.

To make her stays in the country more endurable, for she did have to accompany her husband on occasion to maintain the proper front, Claudia took to inviting an ever-growing entourage of companions. Her very favorite for the moment was her cousin, Helen, a younger woman married to one of the wealthiest lawyers and solicitors in all of Rome. The two women shared a passion for gossip, and both were highly imaginative in indulging themselves in the various pleasures their husbands' status and money could provide. Helen also found horses to be, as she put it, "stimulating," but Claudia managed to overlook that character flaw.

The very first morning after their arrival at Alba Longa, Helen insisted that they go down to view the animals.

"Why?" Claudia moaned, wishing to stay abed awhile longer.

"Because I hope to see them breed, silly! You know how it will put me in the mood for tonight."

"It will be a waste, Helen. There are no available men in this place."

"There are always available men, cousin. Now, come. Up, up, up!"

"It is too, too, too early!"

"Any later and it will be too, too, too hot. Now come. Your husband will be pleased to see you in attendance."

"Your humor evades me."

"Then consider how it will please your son. Last night at dinner he mentioned what a skilled horseman he is becoming. Surely you are interested in the progress of your only son."

"Bitch! You're supposed to be my friend!" Claudia tossed a pillow in Helen's direction. Then, conceding defeat, she picked up a small silver bell and rang it, summoning the maid to draw her bath.

Though it was beyond Claudia's comprehension, just being in the pavilion—before noon, no less—seemed to put her cousin in an exuberant mood. As they settled down onto cushioned benches, Helen pointed to a sleek-muscled stallion.

"Look!" she exclaimed. "See how muscular and strong he appears, yet how smooth and elegant. And see how…" She pointed a manicured finger, then leaned over closer to Claudia and lowered her voice to a whisper.

Though Claudia opened her eyes in mock dismay, she eagerly turned her gaze in the indicated direction. Seeing, her eyes grew even wider. For several moments she stared, her lips parted slightly, then Helen whispered something else that caused her to giggle. In a few moments both women were convulsed with laughter.

In the midst of their frivolity, Steppan came into view, leading a gray and white stallion through the archway that led to the exercise area. He turned and, unlike the other slaves who stoically ignored both the laughter and its source, glanced briefly up toward the grandstand. For a moment the two women were confronted by the living, breathing likeness of one of the statues of a young god so artfully placed about the estate. Then he quickly continued on his way, his finely sculpted torso glistening in the morning sun.

"How magnificent!" Helen exclaimed, rising up slightly to get a better view.

"The horse…or the young attendant?" Claudia teased.

"Both, of course. But I must say, I do prefer the young man."

"Yes," Claudia murmured, completely overlooking Marcellus Servianus, who at that exact moment came riding proudly by on the course below them. "He is a magnificent young animal, isn't he?"

In the ensuing days, the Lady Claudia found herself increasingly preoccupied by the vision of that magnificent young animal. She forced herself to wait a full week, and then went to check on her son's progress again.

The second time she saw the young slave, it occurred to her that he must be the one who had been brought in with the girl Elena, her current wardrobe mistress. But that had been months ago. Perhaps more than a year! How could it be that she had never noticed this one before? She frowned, chastising herself for not visiting the equestrian area more frequently.

The frown gradually transformed itself into a thin smile as she considered that if it had indeed been as long as a year, then she had managed to thwart her husband for that length of time. It had, of course, been clear from the outset that he had marked the new girl to be added to his list of debouchments. But Claudia had blocked his designs by maintaining Elena as an almost constant companion, whether in Rome, at Alba Longa, or when staying with friends.

For years Claudia had been painfully aware of the ongoing series of sexual conquests and intrigues that Lucius Portius engaged in, escapades that were not confined to an occasional affair but rather spiraled until it seemed that women from every rank and station of Rome were included in his adventures. At first she had protested loudly and vehemently. But as time went by, she gradually settled into a state of tight-lipped rancor. Then, as if she had not suffered humiliation enough, the great general and senator had taken to satisfying his lust with slave girls. No longer so interested in—or perhaps capable of—the rituals of seduction, he sought to appease his carnal appetites with those who dared not protest.

But with this last one she had frustrated him—even as he had so often frustrated her by leaving their bed empty and cold through his marauding infidelities.

Now, sitting in the shade of the grandstand at the equestrian area, the Lady Claudia had what she considered a true brainstorm. She had long before taken revenge against her husband's unfaithfulness, and in so doing had extracted double pleasure from her own illicit affairs—though the satisfaction she took from cuckolding Lucius almost inevitably outweighed what she derived from the efforts of her lovers. In time, however, she lost much of what charms she once possessed, and such liaisons seemed increasingly doomed to memory. Now it dawned on her that she might enjoy an ultimate revenge: have not only a splendidly formed young male to train and use exactly as she wished, but in so doing lower what by name belonged to Lucius Cornelius Portius into the same carnal mire he had lowered what belonged to her.

VI

Day after day Steppan fiercely channeled his energy into whatever task lay immediately at hand, forcing himself to relegate anything and everything else to a sort of peripheral blur. Such single-minded focus served to keep him from dwelling overly much on his state and the bleak prospect of ever breaking the invisible bonds that held him, and so it served to block out at least part of the mental anguish of being a slave.

Likewise did such intense focus of effort have its physical rewards. His fierce dedication to each given task at once strengthened his body and drained it of excess energy so that on many nights he slept soundly until dawn.

So it was that Steppan existed, and in some ways—at least in comparison to the storied horrors of the mines and the galleys—he might have seemed more of an apprentice than a slave. He could not deny the reality of what he was, however, not even during those fleeting but blessed nighttime escapes to a far distant place.

Though he had no calendar by which to mark the passing of days, just one month after the anniversary of his arrival at Alba Longa he was pulled aside by Quatro.

"You have no further duties today," Quatro told him. "Rest yourself and eat, then bathe very carefully and put on fresh clothing. Just after sundown I will come for you."

Steppan searched the older man's face anxiously but remained silent.

"There is nothing to fear," Quatro went on steadily. "I will bring you up to the main house. There someone will be waiting. You have only to do as you are told."

As always, Steppan had no choice except to follow orders. Despite Quatro's assurances that he had nothing to fear, Steppan ate without appetite, and his hands shook ever so slightly as he bathed. But he was ready and waiting long before the appointed hour.

Quatro did not appear until after darkness had fallen over the estate. Silently he led Steppan along an unlit path to a shadowed wing of the villa. There he paused and pointed to a doorway. "Knock twice, then enter," he instructed. "You have nothing to fear," he added. Then he turned and quickly became one with the shadows.

For several long moments Steppan stood utterly still, wishing with all his being that he, too, might vanish into the darkness. Instead, he knocked twice, took a deep breath, and tentatively pushed at the door.

Just inside, a woman was waiting. Placing a finger to her lips to indicate that he should remain silent, she ushered him through a courtyard and along a narrow passageway that led to another doorway.

Steppan followed her through the doorway, then stopped short, doubting his senses. The woman who had escorted him to this place appeared to have a dozen identical sisters, all of them shimmering in the torchlight of a seemingly endless chamber. Then it dawned on him: polished mirrors set along the circular walls caught the light of torches and bent it round and round so that the room seemed without end. His vision thus clearing, he saw the deep, wide tub of marble set into the floor, with steps of stone leading down into its depths.

The reflected image of the woman studied him for a moment, directed him to enter the bath, and departed, walking away into the mirrors.

Bewildered, his every sense at full alert, Steppan slowly shed his clothing and, even though he had bathed but a short time before, lowered himself into the bath. The water here was warm, and smelled of flowers. Using the soft cloth draped alongside the rim of marble, he washed again, and then sat waiting, watching himself from different angles.

In a short while the woman reappeared, and, ignoring his embarrassed protests, ordered him out of the tub and into a white towel as large as a robe. When he had dried himself, she motioned him to a couch, knelt beside him, arranged the towel about his loins, and began to massage his body with oil—an act that made him twitch and tingle from the tips of his toes all the way up to the top of his scalp.

When she was finished, she handed him a linen tunic. And after he had slipped into it, she combed his thick dark hair and arranged it carefully about his face. Then she stood back and looked him over appraisingly.

For the first time, Steppan looked at her openly in return. She appeared to be older, yet still attractive. She was well groomed and possessed an air of confidence that told him she must be invested with at least a measure of authority. And yet, he suddenly realized, her true station must be the same as his.

His intuition was essentially correct, for she was indeed a slave, though not quite like himself. She was a Macedonian named Ilene. For many years she had been the Lady Claudia's personal handmaid. The Lady Claudia's deep core of loneliness elevated her long-serving handmaid to be more a servant than a slave. And at times Ilene was almost more of a confidant than a servant. Indeed, other than Quatro, Ilene was the only one who knew of this nocturnal visit. Of course, neither Ilene nor Quatro would even think of speaking of the matter, for they both knew of the tongueless slave who labored in the kitchen, and the manner in which she had lost her instrument of speech.

When her inspection was completed, Ilene allowed a small, unreadable smile, and then conducted Steppan through yet another passageway to yet another door. Here she paused and spoke to him softly.

"Knock thrice, then enter," she said. "The one who awaits you will give you instructions. Do exactly as you are bidden. And never, ever," she cautioned, "say a word of this. Not to anyone. When you leave, it will be as if you had never entered here."

Once again he gathered his breath before entering through an unknown doorway. Once again he found himself in a room such as he had never seen before. But this time it was easier to decipher, for there was no mistaking the furnishings of a bedchamber, no matter how vast and elaborate. Neither was there any mistaking the voice that came from the dark recesses of the bed.

"Extinguish the lamp by the door, young man. Then come to my bed…" the voice commanded, the very same voice he had heard so often of late wafting down—low and husky, like an instrument of music slightly out of tune—from the grandstand overlooking the green and brown pasture of the horse run.

VII

In a dank cave far removed from the splendor of the Portius estate at Alba Longa, the prophet Zebediah sat crouched over a pile of heated stones. Every few minutes he would be seized by a fit of coughing, and then he would bend his body over even more, seeking the dry warmth that arose from the rocks.

With each seizure the men who sat in the cavern with him would look at one another in consternation. Their leader had escaped the Roman ambush at the Jordan, but not unscathed. It was not a physical wound that plagued him, however. And though the flight to safety had entailed several days with little food or water and much exposure to the elements, Zebediah was used to such privation. Rather it was his spirit that was afflicted, sorely wounded by the suffering and loss of life inflicted on so many innocent people. Each day he seemed to sink deeper into sadness, reliving over and over again the terrible sights and sounds of the massacre and scourging himself with blame, for it was because of him so many had come to that place of slaughter.

His appetite, normally slim to begin with, shrank alarmingly; the little sleep he was accustomed to became even less. Then the coughing started and his condition worsened. But for fear of being discovered by the Romans, the men of Zebediah's band dared not move him to one of the towns or villages nearby. In time the Romans would forget—they would have other fish to fry—but for now it was best not to take unnecessary chances. So the small group of frightened men huddled together in the cave, waiting and worrying.

At least one of them was determined to take action, however. If Zebediah's health did not improve soon, Jarel decided, he would take it upon himself to do something, regardless of the danger. Young and blessed with vigor of both body and spirit, and seemingly able beyond the others to grasp the meaning of the teachings and visions of Zebediah, Jarel had become the right hand of the prophet.

So when the coughing seized Zebediah and held him for three full days, Jarel took action. Early on the fourth morning, he descended the hill of the cave. When he returned that evening from a town below, he brought with him a flask of wine mixed with honey and herbs. And by the time the first stars had appeared, the old man was fast asleep.

That night the cave heard no sounds of coughing. Zebediah awoke at sunrise. And for the first time in several days, he left the shelter of the hollowed-out rock and walked alone on the hillside. When he returned to join his followers for breakfast they were greatly relieved, for he appeared clear-eyed and rested.

"A dream came to me during the night," he said, waiting until after they had broken bread to speak. At this announcement the others looked up from their chewing, for when a dream was vivid enough for Zebediah to tell of it, it was usually more than a dream—it was a vision, a message from the Almighty.

"In it," he went on, "a great crowd of people had gathered along the bank of a river. A man whose face I could not see appeared on the far bank. His voice beckoned, and the people began to walk into the water. They descended into the depths until they were covered over. And when they emerged on the opposite side, all of them were spotless and their clothes were the purest white.

"Then…" and here Zebediah paused, looking far away within to recapture whatever it was he had experienced, "…then I heard a voice like thunder proclaim, 'Make ready the way of the Lord!'

"At that, a great hand covered with blood lowered from the heavens down into the water. And when it rose up again, it was washed clean, without a trace of blood.

"And then I awoke."

For some time there was a deep silence within the cave. No one spoke or ate or drank. They scarcely even moved as they awaited an interpretation.

"The voice was so powerful," Zebediah said softly, almost wistfully. "So strong…not at all like my own feeble instrument." He sighed and offered a smile to those gathered around him. "So you see, my brothers, our work is not done after all. Rather, it is just beginning, for the time we have so long awaited is now upon us."

"You mean…?" Jarel began, knowing as did the others huddled together there that the prophet must have been speaking of the advent of the Messiah, the Chosen One. Yet they were unable to truly envision such a wonder coming to pass. For untold generations Jarel's people had heard hollow promises from false prophets, words of deception that left a terrible emptiness in their wake. But the man who sat with them now was no false prophet. On that Jarel would stake his life—as indeed he already had.

The man who had become known only as Zebediah was something of an enigma even to his closest followers. A quiet man of simple tastes and habits, he had been a shepherd for much of his adult life, and he possessed little formal learning. It was not until he reached the advanced age of forty that he had been brought to his calling. The vehicle of his transformation had been a dream, a recurring vision that troubled him deeply. In it there was an open tomb, carved into a hillside of rock. Zebediah entered and saw a roughhewn stone ledge on which there were the unrolled folds of a shroud, but there was no body. As he looked about the tomb in wonder, a voice came from somewhere beyond, uttering a single word...

"Love."

Each time he awoke from the dream, he was greatly disturbed. One night, tormented yet again by the mystery, he cried out in anguish, pleading for the veil to be lifted. At that instant he beheld a solitary star rising in the midnight sky. And when it reached its highest peak, it exploded with a blinding flash, showering light in every direction.

Quaking, Zebediah fell to his knees and covered his eyes. "Lord!" he called out, not knowing what to say or even what power to address. "Lord!"

Once again the unmistakable voice of the tomb came to him, speaking this time from within.

"Love."

"Who are you?" Zebediah cried, thinking that surely his hour had come.

"My name is Love," the voice replied. "And by my name, the darkness of death is conquered. Go now and open the eyes of others, that they might see my light."

Then the voice was gone, and with it the overwhelming brilliance of the light that penetrated Zebediah's upraised hands and tightly closed eyes.

When Zebediah dared to look again, everything about him was as before: the stars were all in place above, and his flock was secure and at rest below. Nonetheless, he was certain that what had been visited upon him was not a dream. Or an illusion. The only uncertainty was why he had been chosen...and how he would go about the task that had been given him.

In the morning he turned his flock over to the man for whom he labored, trusting to the voice within for guidance. From that day forward, Zebediah cast aside concern for his bodily self, for what he would eat and drink, for where he would lay his head at night, for safety and deliverance from peril. Now he was consumed with the message, and with a newfound compassion for his fellow beings, for all the children of the earth regardless of tribe or lineage or allegiance. And his only fear was that their blind eyes would not be opened to the endless flow of light that was life itself.

One Creator, the voice within told him.

One God.

Therefore, all men were brothers. And therefore as well, Zebediah reasoned, the Chosen One, the Messiah, would come to lead not only the children of Israel out of the bondage of darkness, but all humanity as well. This tenet became the basis of his preaching, and though it was a gospel of all-embracing love, a message of universal deliverance and joy, it did not open hearts and minds as he had envisioned, but instead fell most often on ears of stone. For even among his own people, the majority fully expected—even demanded—that the savior they had so long awaited be for them and them alone, the Chosen One for the Chosen People. And to people such as these the words of Zebediah were unwelcome.

Nevertheless, Zebediah spoke what he had been given to speak, and though many rejected him, even reviled and despised him, others both listened and heard, and his followers began to grow in number. So pure were his words, so powerful the simplicity of their message, that they endured after the attack at the River Jordan. As time went by, small groups of people began to gather in secret to discuss the things the prophet had said, and to pray for his return.

Which was exactly what he now planned to do. He would return and go again among the people to spread the words given through him. Only now the message was even more urgent than before, for his own time was swiftly running its course.

"Yes," Zebediah affirmed. "The Chosen One is among us. And so we must go and do the work to which we have been called."

"But...the Romans..." one of the men said, and the looks on the faces of the others showed that they were thinking the same thing.

"You know I will not ask anyone to accompany me if his heart says otherwise," Zebediah answered. "But bear in mind that it is not the Romans—or any other men—that we should fear. Rather, let us fear the Lord...and do the work he has given us to do."

VIII

Though the families of Lucius Portius and Justinian Flavius were loosely linked by birth and more closely by common bonds of wealth and power, Flavius was the first of his household to visit the Portius estate at Alba Longa. Now, as he wound along the wide, stone-lined path in a chariot driven by his bodyguard, he was more than suitably impressed. Perhaps it was the relative newness of the estate, he reflected. Or perhaps he had been away from Rome—and therefore civilization—for so long that he had forgotten what tastefully applied wealth could accomplish. But he could not recall ever viewing a more magnificent setting for a private residence. He had seen larger estates, to be sure, but nothing quite so…elegant.

Yes, that was the word, he decided as the chariot drew up to the villa gleaming with eye-blinking whiteness in the noontime sun. Instead of running toward ostentation, Portius and his architects had created just the right balance of displayed affluence tempered with deliberate understatement, the sum of which translated into a certain ultimate elegance.

As he disembarked the chariot, Flavius reminded himself to suitably mask his admiration, then turned his attention to noting particulars of landscaping and decoration, for his family—in particular his aunt—would have no end of questions.

The doorman ushered him into the library, indicated a table on which a decanter of wine had been placed, and left him temporarily alone. He quenched his thirst. Then, ignoring the hundreds of parchment roll manuscripts carefully arranged to fit the slotted shelves that ran from floor to ceiling along two of the walls, he began to pace about the room, trying to imagine the true purpose of this ostensibly social invitation.

He was not given long to speculate. In a matter of minutes, Lucius Portius came striding through the door, fixed an appraising eye on his young visitor, and extended both arms in greeting.

"Ah, Tribune!" he exclaimed, making reference to Justinian's new rank. "How you have matured! I scarcely recognized you!"

"But I have no difficulty in recognizing you, General," Justinian replied. "Time has indeed smiled upon you."

"I have managed to keep that ancient thief somewhat at bay," Portius allowed, not at all displeased with the compliment. "Please…" He motioned Justinian to a chair, picked up a tiny bell from his desk, and waved it. Almost instantly a girl bearing a tray of fruit and wine appeared.

The new tribune looked up casually at the interruption, then took a second look. The girl was taller than average, and very well proportioned—a dark-haired, dark-eyed morsel clad in a long but nearly transparent gown that molded to her every movement. Placing the tray on the table, she bowed ever so slightly in the direction of her master and departed, carefully avoiding a direct glance at either man.

"You approve?" Portius asked, looking over at Flavius from behind his desk with a probing smile.

The younger man flushed slightly. "Ah…" he began, somewhat embarrassed for having allowed himself to stare so openly. "Ah…yes. I must say, you have a most discriminating eye."

"At one time I had thought to make her a wardrobe mistress for my Claudia," Portius said. "But she proved to be too high-spirited for my lady's liking. So in the end, I, ah, retrained her and made her a serving wench. Personally, I find her spirit not at all disagreeable."

"Yes…" Flavius replied, not at all certain as to how he should react. "That is, I should imagine not."

Several moments ensued without any further conversation. When Portius calculated that his guest was becoming just uneasy enough, he broke the silence with polite inquiries about the health and welfare of various Flavius family members, received appropriately polite answers, and then abruptly shifted to the business at hand.

"You may have wondered at the reason for your sudden recall from Judea," he remarked.

Justinian Flavius took a carefully measured sip of wine before answering.

"As a soldier of Rome, I stand ready to go without question where my commander directs me," he intoned. "But of course it is only natural to have given the matter some thought. Now that you mention it, did you by chance play a hand in the transfer?"

"Let us say that I had some small measure of influence..."

"Well, then, let me offer you my sincere thanks. I personally found Judea to be a wretched place."

"The life of a soldier is not always a pleasant one," Portius observed dryly. "Nor perhaps should it be. But in your case, I thought your talents would be better utilized closer to home. So I helped persuade certain individuals that the garrison of Rome had need of your service."

"The garrison of Rome!" Justinian Flavius sat bolt upright, unable to conceal either his surprise or his delight. "I...well, that's quite an honor! But, if I may be so bold as to ask, why do you bestow this post on me?

Portius gave an almost imperceptible shrug. "In truth, there are several reasons. First and foremost, our families have long been bonded in friendship. As a matter of fact, I have a certain debt of friendship to your father, which, since his unfortunate passing, I felt I might be able to discharge through you." He paused, measuring the young man seated before him. "And, of course, perhaps we might be of mutual benefit to one another."

"Of course. I would be most pleased to do whatever I might to repay your...interest in my career."

"I appreciate your spirit of cooperation," Portius said. "But repayment is not at all necessary. As I said, I have the debt to discharge. Besides, what I propose is simple enough and, as mentioned, is offered in the spirit of being of service to one another. There is, however, one thing of which I must make you aware at the outset. The post with the garrison of Rome will be a temporary one."

Aware that he was being tested, though for what purpose he could not begin to fathom, Justinian Flavius did his best to remain impassive. Whatever old Portius was up to, he would soon enough find out. Meanwhile, he had need of any measure of aid the man might provide, especially now, since his father had died and the Flavius family fortunes had become so suddenly and incredibly precarious.

"But the eventual rewards will more than compensate," Portius went on. "The situation at hand is this: I wish for my son, Marcellus Servianus, to pursue a career in the military. Not on a permanent basis, you understand, but as a means of acquiring a certain training and experience that will serve him well later on in life. Much as you, yourself, are doing. Unfortunately, while Marcellus is a very bright lad, he shows little inclination at all toward the military. It is my hope, therefore, that in time you would take him under your tutelage, so to speak. Make him your personal aide. A young officer such as yourself could be of considerable help and guidance to someone like Marcellus. And, naturally, such help would not go unappreciated."

"I understand," Flavius said, though in fact he did not have the slightest idea why Portius was so determined to thrust his son into a career, no matter how temporary, for which the boy apparently had neither aptitude nor liking. With the vast Portius fortune and the power it spawned, Marcellus Servianus could embark on virtually any path he chose and still be assured of all possible success.

Lucius Portius nodded approvingly. "Good. Now then, I sensed your disappointment at the mention of a temporary stay with the city garrison. But consider that while such a position is undoubtedly attractive, it may not be best for a young man seeking the heights to stay there overlong. You might in time desire a command of your own, for example. Or you might wish to occupy a place in the senate, beside your uncle. Not, of course, that you or your family are in need of my help in such matters…"

"Your help is both welcome and valuable," Flavius quickly assured his host.

"Then we are agreed?"

"Yes, sir. We are agreed."

"Excellent!" Portius arose and gestured toward the outdoors. "Would you care to accompany me to the stables before we have lunch? I would value your opinion on a mare I recently purchased." He started to lead the way, then paused and turned about. "By the way, you are prepared to spend the night, aren't you? It is, after all, a long journey back home."

"Yes, of course. I would be delighted to spend the night," Flavius replied, for while he was less than at ease in the presence of his host, there were things to be explored here.

"Splendid! Splendid! I have a little something in mind that will hopefully add to your delight," Portius said, smiling to himself. The young tribune's reaction to the serving girl had provided the necessary key to his inclinations, but he would not be favored with that particular girl after all. No, it would be much more interesting to present him with that which the master of the villa had been unable to claim for himself. Of course, Claudia would no doubt soon enough discover what had happened, and she would loudly disapprove, but it would be after the fact. At any rate, she would have to at least pretend to overlook the matter out of consideration for family ties. And, best of all, once the deed had been accomplished, the door of resistance broken down, then he, too, would be able to enter.

After the long journey to Alba Longa, the subtle tension underlying the sociability of the day, and the fullness of the evening meal (There had been just four courses, but each one was superb: first a medley of salads, mushrooms, and sardines; then a light and excellent mackerel surrounded by an assortment of prawns; next a delicately roasted pheasant accompanied by a hearty venison; and finally a choice of desserts so rich and varied that the last of the wines scarcely had room in which to flow), Justinian Flavius wearily sought the quiet repose of his bedchamber. It was with a measure of irritation, therefore, that he answered a knock at the door.

"A token of my hospitality," Lucius Portius muttered when the door was opened. "Her name is Elena. She is yours for the night. Do exactly with her as you please." He thrust the young woman into the room, turned and walked unsteadily away.

After he recovered from his initial surprise, Flavius's first thought was that if he was going to be presented with a bed partner, he would have preferred the tall, dark-haired girl who had served him in the library. However, on closer inspection, this wench seemed appetizing enough: blonde hair, full bosom, strong but feminine features.

"Well, I do appreciate the noble gesture of my host, and you are an attractive young thing, but it has been a long and tiring day. So…" he motioned toward the bed in a jaded, off-handed manner as if to suggest that it was his duty rather than hers that must be performed.

Elena did not move. Before the beast with the whip, no man had lain with her—not any of the clan, or any other. Nor had any man since, not even the one rich beyond belief who had bought her. And neither would this one, who thought to use her in the sacred way with no more thought than he would give to draining another cup before falling off to sleep.

"Come!" Flavius commanded, and when the girl still did not respond, he reached out and pulled her roughly to the couch. "Perhaps you have been trained to tease!" he rasped, suddenly aroused by her reluctance—and the perverted thought that Portius, who knew so well the pleasures of the flesh, might well have sent him a girl skilled in the pretense of shyness. "Well," he leered, shoving her down and falling atop her, "show me your talents, then!"

Elena suffered his first caresses in silence, trying desperately to look beyond the moment, for only by thinking clearly would she have any hope of deliverance. And yet she knew that ultimately there would be no deliverance. If it was not this nameless stranger it would be another, for the man who had bought her had told her as much. If she would not come to him willingly, he threatened, he would give her to those who would take her by force: to houseguest, to bodyguard, to stable hand, eventually to two or three at a time. Only by offering her master with complete submission that prize he so mindlessly craved would she gain his protection. But even with that empty promise she would still be but a slave, would merely be purchasing time in a living hell.

She had thought of all this a hundred times before, and always she had arrived at the same decision. So when Justinian Flavius began to explore her most feminine parts, she reacted without need of further thought. Thrusting his hand away, she brought her own up in a quick rising arc that ended in a stinging slap against his cheek.

So unthinkable was this act that for several long moments Flavius crouched above her in unmoving disbelief. Tentatively, almost fearfully, he touched at the place where she had struck him. Then he retaliated.

"Bitch!" he snarled, striking her with the flat of his hand. "So this is what Portius has sent me! A teasing..." again he struck her "...barbarian..." and again "...bitch!"

A trickle of blood issued from Elena's nose, but she made no effort to avoid the blows. Nor, except for the first strike, did she make any outcry, for in turning away to avoid it she had glimpsed an instrument of deliverance. And if she could reach it, what she had to endure in the meantime did not really matter.

"So!" Flavius panted, satisfied that she would offer no further resistance. "You remember your place after all!" He rolled off the couch and stood over her. "Now, do exactly as you are told. Exactly...and I may forget to mention your behavior to your master. Do you understand?"

Elena nodded silently.

"Good. First, wipe your nose. Blood nauseates me. And then...take off your clothes..."

Closing her eyes so that she would not have to see him watching, Elena did as she was told. But though she could not see his reaction, she heard it all too clearly: first in his rapid, strangled breathing and then in his words, words strange to her but understood just the same, words vile and abusive and degrading by their very tone.

"Now, open your eyes so that you may view the prize you are about to receive," Flavius taunted. "Who knows, you might enjoy a younger man for a change…"

Now thoroughly aroused, he yanked his tunic up over his head, but in his haste he got it tangled about his shoulders. He uttered a string of oaths, but they did not budge the cloth by so much as an inch.

The target was so open and inviting that she acted on pure impulse. Quickly grasping the instrument of her deliverance—the dagger that lay just beyond Justinian's pillow—she drove the point of it into his pale, naked buttocks.

He felt one leg inexplicably give way, and then came the sharp, ripping pain that brought forth a tunic-muffled cry. Collapsing to the floor, he clawed frantically at the garment, shrieking and howling and cursing.

Despite her deadly predicament, Elena nearly burst out laughing as she watched the young Roman thrashing about on the floor. But she quickly steadied herself. The first thrust had not only been delivered to the wrong place, no matter how tempting, it had been far too weak. The next one must have both strength and purpose.

Justinian Flavius freed himself of the tunic and struggled to get to his feet, shrieking and howling anew as he became aware of the flow of his own precious blood.

Clutching the hilt with both hands, Elena turned the blade and plunged it with all her might into her own yielding breast. She heard more than felt it strike something solid, then pushed on through to the underlying softness. The young Roman was rising unsteadily to his feet, a look of horror in his bulging eyes. Then the pain came with a searing, wrenching force, and she wanted to cough but could not. Her legs would not hold her anymore, and in the swiftly fading torchlight there was something flowing and warm, and the Roman was sliding back down to the floor.

IX

"Sell him to me," Helen whispered, giggling with lascivious delight.

"You know I cannot," Claudia whispered back, not taking her eyes off the object of their conversation, who just then had been halted by Quatro as he was about to lead a horse past the grandstand and out to the exercise area.

"Surely you could part with one single slave," Helen persisted, shading her eyes against the glare of the morning sun and the wine of the evening before. "Why, you have so many slaves running about that one more or less would not even be noticed."

"This one is different," Claudia countered, already questioning the wisdom of having confided in her cousin. "My husband has great plans for him."

"Your husband?" Helen arched one of her eyebrows theatrically, a talent Claudia had practiced diligently in front of her mirror but never managed to duplicate. "My dear, I thought you had the great plans!"

Helen had arrived back at Alba Longa the previous evening after an absence of several months, coming in answer to Claudia's plea that the monotony of life there was becoming unbearable. And even before they were at dinner, Claudia had eagerly intimated certain details of her latest, and most naughty, indiscretion. Actually, she had more exaggerated than hinted, for though Steppan had been summoned to her chambers three times in nearly twice that many months, the Lady Claudia having been obliged to be in Rome for much of that time and exceedingly discreet when in residence at the country estate, she made it seem by the telling as if a passionate young demi-god visited her almost nightly to fulfill her every demand for pleasure.

"It's out of the question," Claudia replied somewhat stiffly. "The young… horseman…should be occupied here for quite some time."

"Well, then..." Helen sighed, plucking at a cluster of figs in a bowl beside her. "Perhaps you might arrange something else for your lonely little cousin. Perhaps that handsome young officer who was at dinner last night."

"Justinian Flavius."

"Yes, that's the one."

"His uncle is Tertullius Flavius."

"Oh, how delightful! Rich as well as good-looking! Will he be down to view the horses today?"

"I expected that he and my husband would have been here long before now. Shall I send to inquire?"

"No, don't bother. But he does prefer women, doesn't he? I mean, everyone is aware that some of the Flavius family..."

"There are certain things you must find out for yourself, my dear cousin," Claudia answered gaily, beginning to wonder what was keeping Steppan and Quatro so earnestly engaged in conversation.

Though he knew of the incident before daybreak, Quatro waited until midmorning before speaking of it to Steppan. Drawing the youth aside, he repeated what he had heard: Elena had been found dead, by her own hand.

Steppan's eyes registered a moment of furious denial, and then went blank.

"I could say that you are sick..." Quatro said, offering to release him from the day.

It was a monumental gesture, one which Steppan would later appreciate all the more. But for the moment he merely shook his head, his grip tight about the reins of the horse he held.

"No," he muttered after a while, turning to lead the horse away. "When I am sick enough, they will know." Then he heard a familiar, whiny voice.

Marcellus Servianus Portius was among the unhappiest of all young men. It had been a constant and chafing indignity that his father persisted in treating him like a child—insisting, for example, that he spend much of the entire summer at Alba Longa, away from his friends in Rome, engaged in such tedious and useless pursuits as learning to train a horse and aim an arrow, all under the direction of a slave no older than himself!

Still, he had endured, had straddled the uncomfortable beast and pulled back the insubordinate bowstring until backside and fingers alike were calloused and sore, hoping to convince his father that he was no longer a mere youth but had grown into a man.

And what had been his reward for all his persistent efforts? The very evening before, his father had informed him, without any prior discussion or consultation, that he was soon to be put under the military tutelage of Justinian Flavius. It was a stroke of good fortune, the old man had beamed, having a friend of the family to act as personal mentor, adding expansively that when the time came to depart, Marcellus could have his pick of both horse and manservant to accompany him, no doubt hoping to pacify by this pathetic display of generosity.

Right then and there Marcellus Servianus decided that since the general insisted that he learn the arts of war, he would begin immediately by launching a campaign of resistance. His first act of defiance was to sit stonily throughout the ensuing meal, pointedly ignoring his food. But his father was so immersed in conversation with Flavius that he took no notice whatsoever of the hunger strike.

After a night of fitful sleep, Marcellus arose more incensed than ever. As he walked to the site of his daily torment, he conceded defeat on his opening strategy. He obviously could not withstand a prolonged siege without food, and his father was so preoccupied with his own affairs that he seemed entirely oblivious to both the refusal to eat and the stony wall of silence that surrounded it. Therefore, Marcellus resolved to embark on a new plan of battle.

So engrossed was the younger Portius with thoughts of this new tactic that he failed to perceive the tight ring of tension that encompassed the equestrian area like a second fence. Amazingly enough, neither did he notice his mother and his Aunt Helen sitting in the shaded area of the grandstand. And so, following his revised plan, he informed Quatro that he would practice archery first that day and attend to riding and work with the sword later.

When the target had been dutifully set up, Marcellus stretched the bowstring tight, took careful aim, and sent the arrow sailing high above the mark and into the trees beyond. Without pause he notched a second arrow and sent that one into the ground a mere three paces in front of his own feet. Half a dozen times in a row he aimed and shot without once threatening even the edge of the target. Then, satisfied, he turned and thrust the bow out to Steppan in an imperious gesture.

"Enough! I feel off the mark today," he declared, smirking with self-satisfaction at his play on words.

Silent and impassive as ever, Steppan reached out his hand.

Just as Steppan touched the bow, Marcellus Servianus drew it back again. "On second thought," he said, seized with a sudden inspiration, "I'll have one more try. I feel a new surge of confidence."

Now he would give them all a lesson, he told himself. One they would not soon forget! He selected a sharp-tipped arrow from the quiver, fitted it to the bow, then quickly swept about and took aim at a new target.

It was the first good shot he had ever made. The arrow sped to its mark straight and strong and true, found the neck of a tall, finely muscled gray and white stallion and pierced it deeply, sending the splendid animal rearing skyward then plunging toward the ground.

Only when he turned again and saw the thunderstruck look on the faces of Quatro and Steppan did Marcellus Servianus begin to comprehend the rashness of his act. O great Jupiter! he silently shouted. He had killed one of his father's beloved horses! One of his finest thoroughbreds!

Tears of panic stung his eyes. He shook his head, trying to think his way out of the predicament. He could say that it had been an accident. Yes, an accident. One of the slaves, indeed, the very same one who had been chosen especially to tutor him, had led the animal into the path of the arrow. It was the slave called Steppan who was to blame! Then he heard a commotion in the grandstand and raised his eyes to see his mother there, and his Aunt Helen, and knew there was no way around his father's wrath! The slaves might have been dealt with, and it was possible his mother would have protected him. But not Helen! Never Helen! She would embellish the smallest detail, seen and unseen alike!

"Here!" he snarled, holding the bow at arm's length with shaking hand, his anger all the more intense because it was self-directed. But this time Steppan made no move to take it.

"Slave!" Marcellus bellowed, quaking with fright-stoked rage. "Take my bow!"

Still Steppan did not move; he stood absolutely motionless, as if he had not even heard.

"How dare you!" Marcellus sputtered, now completely beside himself. Lips quivering, fingers trembling, he struggled to fit yet another arrow to his bowstring. "I'll show you, damn you! You filthy, dirty swine!"

Blinking against the stream of frustration coursing down his cheeks, he brought the bow to position. From the very first it had been painfully evident that everyone—his father, the slave Quatro, even his mother!—thought that this new boy, this new slave, was actually superior. Better with horses! Better with the sword! Better with the bow! Stronger! Swifter! Braver! Oh, they had tried to hide their thoughts, had made sure to offer lukewarm compliments on his own progress, but he had seen the truth behind their lies. Well, now they would see what this Steppan truly was: A slave! Nothing but a stinking, rotten slave!

And now a dead one!

All his life Quatro had been a slave. He was born the son of a slave, was reared in slavery, and would die without ever knowing life as a free man. Thus it was that he stood transfixed, rooted in his heritage, until the final moment. When at last he did move, he came as close as he ever had to breaking the invisible chains that had so long held him, but it was too late. Screaming a final curse, Marcellus Servianus turned the bow on Steppan and let the arrow loose.

Steppan was more than a dozen feet away, but he saw what was coming. That and his superb reflexes saved him. As he dropped to the ground, he felt the tip of the arrow sting his shoulder in passing. Not born to slavery himself, neither yet too long a slave, he immediately sprang up and forward, swept the bow away with one hand, and with the other delivered a single, smashing blow that crumpled the soft patrician face.

It was the first time in all his life that Marcellus Servianus had ever been struck. So startled was he by the sudden and unprecedented attack that he made no effort at all to defend himself, not that it would have made any difference. Afterward he would recall that he had felt a heavy and palpable rush—as if a dense wall of wind was descending upon him—as the slave leapt forward. But at the actual moment, he was aware only of the two eyes gleaming with a demon's fury and the fist that seemed to emerge from between them.

X

Why? Why? Why! Lucius Cornelius Portius picked up a goblet and threw it angrily against the library wall, then watched in horror as the fermented juice of grapes splashed over a row of rare parchment manuscripts.

"Damn it!" he shouted, now doubly incensed. He grabbed a silver bell from his desk and rang it, and then he forced himself to be seated while a servant came in and cleaned up the mess.

The moment the slave departed, Portius began to pace agitatedly about the room again.

Despite his enormous wealth and his great political power, he was as much a stranger to happiness as was his son. Though he had long been possessed of riches far in excess of any conceivable need, his whole existence had nevertheless become a ceaseless quest for more, a daily bout of scheming and planning, buying and selling, bargaining and fixing that sealed him off from peace and contentment. Now, at the height of his worldly powers, the foremost pleasure all his efforts had brought him was centered about the stables at Alba Longa. There alone had he been able to purchase any semblance of tranquility.

But even that had been shattered. In the last day and a half it seemed as if the gods had all turned against him at once.

First there had been that embarrassing business with Justinian Flavius. Of course, it was unthinkable that the girl would have taken her own life rather than entertain a guest. And unthinkable as well that Flavius would have allowed such a thing to happen. Not that anyone knew exactly what had taken transpired. Except Flavius, of course, and what he had to say was both sketchy and entirely defensive. He must have been quite drunk, Portius concluded, though he had seemed well enough in control at dinner.

At any rate, young Flavius had a stab wound in his backside and the potential breath of a scandal hanging over his head. Not that the term *scandal* would ordinarily be applied to an affair involving a slave. But in this case there would certainly be conjecture, which would in turn become gossip, and gossip had a way of transforming the most trivial event into an epic of iniquity and disgrace. Not that Portius found the matter in the least amusing. Far from it. Flavius was a guest in his house, and it was therefore more than unfortunate that Flavius had suffered injury; it was an embarrassment to the Portius family as well.

Of course the girl's death had been most untimely. Not once had he the pleasure of knowing her body, and now he never would.

Then there was the stallion. That magnificent animal! Dead! Wasted! And an expensive waste it was, for the horse had cost far more than the girl. What in the name of the gods had possessed Marcellus to do such a thing? Portius silently raged, taking such inexcusable action was even further proof of the wisdom—no, the necessity—of placing the boy in the military. The discipline provided there would be precisely what was needed.

Last but by no means least was the incident with the slave boy. Whatever the cause, a slave could not be allowed to strike his master or any member of his master's family. That was a matter of principle—time-honored and immutable. If the boy had been content to merely hold Marcellus off, the situation might have been easily resolved. But as it now stood, the episode called for serious and immediate punishment. Even death.

Lucius Portius uttered an explosive string of oaths. The girl was dead, and that was a costly and disturbing waste.

The stallion was dead, and that was another waste, and an even greater expense.

It made no good sense, then, to have this other slave killed and so incur a third waste of flesh and money. Perhaps he could have the boy severely beaten and let it go at that, Portius thought, searching for a way out. Then he quickly dismissed the idea, for it would both show weakness and set a dangerous precedent. Still and all, he could not tolerate being thrice a loser.

Then, as he paced about the library of his villa at Alba Longa, cursing the rapid chain of events that had that caused his chest to tighten like a clamp about his heart and lungs, Portius stumbled onto a masterful idea. There was a way to recoup some of his investment after all, he suddenly realized, stopping in mid-stride. He knew of a place firsthand where a young male slave such as

Steppan could be sent that would provide not only satisfactory punishment, but a measure of monetary recompense as well.

The deep-etched scowl and snarling lips relaxed into the beginning of a smile as Portius sat down and began to scrawl a message on parchment. When he was finished, he sealed the letter with wax and rang the silver bell again.

"Have this delivered," he instructed. "And have my driver wait for a message in return."

Though he was born on the wrong side of the socio-economic fence, Antonius Cappio had managed to rise from the fringe of poverty to a position of considerable wealth in a short period of time.

Arena fighting had become the rage of Rome. Male and female, young and old, rich and poor, soldier, tradesman, farmer, businessman, courtesan, politician, and especially those on the dole all flocked to the spectacle of arena play in ever-increasing numbers. Arenas began to spring up everywhere—not only in the cities, but also in small towns and villages. Rather than reaching a peak and then quickly dying out, the fever for violence and bloodshed by proxy rose ever higher. And with it grew the prospects for profit in the market for flesh to occupy the theaters of blood.

Antonius Cappio, eldest son of a poor farmer, had left the rocky hillside of his family home near Capua at an early age to test his fortunes in the Mother City, Rome. Starting in back streets and alleys, he hustled, gambled, and organized a collection of street toughs into an association that provided a crude form of insurance under the name of protection. He made political alliances that progressed from shady to marginal to respectable, and eventually became a valued solicitor for certain prominent lawyers. All the while, he searched for that grand scheme that would carry him to the riches that he knew in his bones was his destiny.

On the death of his father, he journeyed back to the family habitat, surveyed its sparseness, and knew he had found that destiny. Using cheap local labor, he converted the barn to living quarters and constructed a flimsy wooden arena. He then went back to Rome, sold what business interests he had there, and purchased two male slaves at auction and two condemned criminals from a friendly jailer—acquiring one of the latter virtually without cost because he was speechless, a defect that mattered little for the purpose Cappio had in mind.

Promising his ragged quartet their eventual freedom if they worked well, he established his fighting school: four desperate and unskilled gladiators, his sisters to cook and clean and tend to wounds, his brother to serve as guard and assistant trainer, and himself to juggle the hats of owner, manager, trainer, promoter, and financier.

Through a blend of the owner's relentless hard work, political maneuvering, and gritty determination—not to mention being in the right place at the right time—the enterprise flourished beyond all expectations. Word of the little arena at Capua spread rapidly, and soon extra seats had to be installed in the arena and the barn living quarters expanded to accommodate new gladiators. Cappio's had intended to promote point matches, avoiding matches to the death until he had a more abundant supply of talent. And so he had not anticipated an immediate need for more fighters. However, as he soon learned, what took place on the arena floor was often unpredictable.

The first casualty came when the mute suffered a sliced hamstring, which ended his service. Then the hurriedly purchased replacement was run through the chest by a sword wielded by the very same fighter who had ended the career of the mute.

Ever the optimist, Cappio consoled himself with the thought that at least he had one good fighter. And so he persevered.

In due time his school for gladiators became one of the largest and most elaborate anywhere in the empire. Where once there were but two pairs to be matched, and sad ones at that, there were now two dozen well-trained dealers of death. In place of the old irregular lean-to grandstand, there now stood an imposing circular structure that provided seating for three hundred, with private boxes for the wealthy and privileged.

The barn had been replaced by a barracks that housed narrow cells in which the gladiators slept, an eating hall, and a bath. At one end of the barracks was an exercise yard—a rectangle of hard-packed dirt two hundred feet long by eighty-five feet wide surrounded by a high fence surmounted by sharpened spikes. And at the opposite end, a courtyard led to the kitchen and beyond that to quarters for the trainers and guards. There was also a separate building for the female slaves who were kept to, among other duties, service the more successful gladiators. His fighters were given the best of everything, Cappio was fond of boasting: the best training, the best food…and the best women.

Cappio had not neglected his own comfort and pleasure while expanding his business. The family hut had been supplanted by a spacious villa, a house of many rooms and luxuries, with gardens and pools and orchards—rows and rows of trees laden with more fruit in one season than he and his gang had managed to steal from the markets in all his years in Rome.

His sisters had married, as had his brother. But Cappio remained a bachelor, the solitary master of a swelling retinue of slaves to look after his household needs.

There was even a private corps of guards, a collection of retired soldiers augmented from time to time by members of the Roman garrison headquartered at Capua.

All in all, Antonius Cappio was well pleased with the way of life he had constructed for himself, and on those rare occasions when he paused to consider that it was a life built on pillars of enforced servitude and the specter of death, he overrode such thoughts with the rejoinder that if one had to be a slave, then the life of a gladiator was among the best a man could hope for. There was decent housing and nourishing food, and success brought a certain fame and glory, sometimes even silver as well. And exceptional success carried with it the chance to gain the gift of freedom.

Yes, the life of a gladiator was among the best a slave could hope for, just as the life of a successful fighting school owner was among the best of existences a man such as himself could hope for—a man not born to wealth and its privileges, a man who had to take the world into which he had been born and mold it to his liking.

As if to provide proof of his personal success, one of the richest and most powerful men in all of Rome was now seated before him, having come in person to discuss a business proposal.

"I am honored by your presence," Cappio said, after looking over the proffered goods, "but I'm afraid he is too young to be of value here."

"Ah, but his youth is to your advantage," Lucius Portius countered. "That gives you all the more time to train him to perfection. I make no exaggeration, Antonius, when I tell you this one has truly exceptional potential for use here. In fact, I am confident in saying that if you bring him along carefully, as only you know how, you will find your investment repaid many times over."

Cappio leaned the weight of his elbows on his desk, a delicately fashioned piece inlaid with strips of polished gold, and cupped his chin in his hands as if weighing the proposal, though he knew full well there was little to consider. The man before him was not only very rich and influential, he was a very good customer.

"Ah, well..." Cappio sighed at last, lifting his gaze from the desk, "it's just as they say: The rich get richer."

A thin smile creased the lean, patrician face of Cappio's visitor. "Spare me the aphorisms," he said. "From the look of things, it seems you have not done so badly for yourself."

"Fate has been kind to me," Cappio allowed. "I only hope that the gods continue to smile on me by allowing your prediction about my latest investment to come to pass."

"So, we are agreed then?" Portius asked.

"Yes, we are agreed."

"Splendid! Then we can proceed to our next order of business, that of arranging for an afternoon's entertainment."

XI

"Come!" The man uttered just the one word, then turned and led the way. As they crossed an open area where men were practicing with wooden swords and daggers under the watchful eyes of trainers armed with weapons of steel, he slowed his pace and looked back, expecting the newcomer to slow or even stop to watch. To his surprise, the youth was so closely on his heels that he nearly collided with him.

"So," the man said. "What do you think?" He was obviously a man of considerable physical power, thickset and ruggedly muscled, and no stranger to combat and pain. His nose was broad from having been broken, one ear was misshapen and hammered against the side of his skull, and a latticework of scars crisscrossed his chest and one shoulder.

"Nothing," the youth answered, not understanding what he was seeing.

For a moment the man's dark eyes probed the unlined face of the newcomer. Then he nodded ever so slightly to himself, as if a deeper question had been answered.

"Good," he said.

The newcomer was taken to the barracks and shown the pallet he was to occupy.

"Tonight you will eat with the others," the man said. "In the morning you will be assigned your duties."

Then he was left alone.

Or nearly so.

"I see you've met Braccus."

Seated on a nearby pallet with his back against the wall was a curly-haired youngster whose smooth cheeks and chin identified him as still more boy than man in age.

"The one who brought you here," the curly-haired one went on, new to this strange place himself and eager to talk. Especially to someone near his own age. "He's the head trainer. A freedman."

"Freedman?"

"Yes. He was once a slave, but he won his freedom in the arena. It is said he was the best and most fierce fighter ever seen in Capua. And yet he still walks newcomers down here himself. Why, I don't know."

"Arena? What is this arena?"

"The arena is a place where men fight."

The newcomer pondered this, envisioning the wrestling matches and other contests of strength and skill held by the clan during feasts and festivals. "Those men back there. In the big open space. They had swords and knives that looked to be made of wood…"

"They were training. Practicing their weapons."

"Are they warriors?"

"You don't know, do you?"

"What?"

"Where you have come to."

"No."

The curly haired one sighed. "Then let me be the one to tell you…"

Before he entered there, Steppan had not known such a place existed, nor that there were men trained to deliver death and receive it, not to protect family and loved ones or clan or tribe, nor for honor or glory, but for the entertainment… the amusement…the idle pleasure of others.

Because he was yet too young for the arena, he was put to use cleaning the barracks and the training yard and repairing equipment. From the corner of his labors he watched the men called gladiators with a sort of fascinated horror. As a group they were hard, quick, powerful—and subject to a discipline almost too terrible to bear, though they had their individual differences, as did all men. Some of them walked through their daily hell with vacant and silent stares; some made their way swaggering and raucous and boastful; and a few seemed to look forward to that sickening moment when they would face a fellow unfortunate in combat and so rid themselves of some part of their raging fear and hatred by thrusting it onto another.

And some, unable to exist with the knowledge of what they had become and the destiny that awaited them, chose not to walk any longer at all. In the second month he was at Capua, the new youth saw one man drop his weapons and run shrieking and cursing and clawing at the high iron bars surround the training area, embracing the oblivion awaiting him.

Though he tried to block them, unbidden thoughts soon came to haunt him. Horrible images of the dreadful moment of his own trial: the gut wrenching anticipation…the trembling steps out onto the arena floor, his being so nakedly exposed…his opponent towering over him, clad in the impenetrable armor of experience…the paralyzing shrill blast of the trainer's whistle…the terrible thrust and hacks of the sword, the razor-like slices of the dagger…his flesh ripped opened…his blood gushing forth…his life draining before the fat, rich, greedy eyes of those who had bought with coins of wealth and power the spectacle so gross and ultimately degrading that no creature of land or sea or air save that which walked upright on two legs and went by the name of Roman could conceive and carry out.

As a means of defense against such horrors, he built up an even greater fortress of duty and work than before, embracing each task no matter how tedious or low with a zeal that was akin to gratitude, for the more he could immerse himself in physical labor, the more he could avoid dialogues with himself.

Strong, Quatro had said.

Be strong.

Yes…he would be strong.

So he wrapped himself in a tight cycle of mindless toil, day becoming night becoming day becoming night over and over again without the slightest ray of light or laughter.

Antonius Cappio listened attentively as Braccus delivered his report. "So," he said, when Braccus was finished, "we substitute the Thracian from the mines, the one with the crooked nose, for the Jew who lost a finger, and we still have three matched pairs ready for Saturday's event?"

"Yes," Braccus confirmed.

"And the Jew? Has he recovered from his injury?"

"Yes. If anything, he is meaner than ever. I think he's actually looking forward to stepping out onto the arena floor. As long as it's a matter of points, that is."

"I myself would be pleased if it were always a matter of points," Cappio said. "But the fact is that people are willing to pay the price to see matches to the final conclusion. So what are we to do? In the end, we must give the customer what the customer wants." He sighed and shook his head solemnly, as if truly regretting the injustice of it all.

Braccus waited without replying, and Cappio, not totally insensitive to the fact that this valued and trusted employee standing before him had endured a number of afternoons "to the conclusion," moved on to his main concern.

"And the youth that came in some months ago? The curly haired one from Gaul?"

Braccus gave a negative shake of his head. "He has neither skills nor stomach for the arena. Perhaps you could set him to work in the kitchen. Or landscaping."

Cappio frowned, moving a jeweled ring slowly back and forth over the flesh of his pudgy index finger. "What about the other one? The barbarian boy?"

"Ah, that's another story. That one shows promise."

"Oh? When I viewed him he seemed so young."

"Young, yes. But he is more man than boy. I think that one was born more man than boy."

The frown vanished, the ring stilled. "Tell me about him…"

"He is disciplined. He works hard and speaks little. He eats what is put before him and he seems to sleep well. And he watches…"

"He watches?"

"He observes, but without appearing to observe. I have seen him mimic the training of the others. He is strong and quick, and he does the movements with precision."

"What else," Cappio prompted, sensing there was more.

"Well, there is something I feel, not see. As young as he is, I sense a breath of danger about him."

"A breath of danger…" The sliver of a smile formed on Cappio's lips as he considered within himself. Perhaps some of what Lucius Portius had said would prove to be true. Perhaps this young barbarian was, indeed, possessed of exceptional abilities. If so, the coins that had been transferred to Portius's hands just might be repaid over and over again.

"I think it's time I took a closer look at this one myself," Cappio said. "Send him to the training yard in the morning and put him through some beginning exercises."

"Yes, sir. Anything else?"

"No, nothing else. You have done well, Braccus."

Braccus straightened and gave the gladiator's salute, one clenched fist clasped to his chest, and then turned about and went back to his duties. Cappio made his decision in half an hour of firsthand observation, and he ordered the young barbarian transferred from the tedium of cleaning the barracks and yard to the regimen of training.

Now Steppan began each day with a grueling series of exercises designed to increase his quickness, strength, and endurance, though at first they seemed to drain him of those very attributes. By midmorning such drills would be finished, and, his body already lathered with sweat, he would be set to work with the tools of his future trade. Training at first with wooden dagger and blunted sword, he gained knowledge of the distinct and peculiar art of these and other weapons in turn as he progressed through the gladiator's arsenal, learning to dodge, feint, parry, thrust, attack…to kill without being killed.

The newest addition to the gladiator corps proved to be a remarkably adept pupil. Fighting became a natural outlet through which his constant inner turmoil could be at least temporarily released. And there was something else: he had heard that if a man fought well enough, and survived long enough, he might earn his freedom. This was evidenced by Braccus, who was known to be a freedman yet preferred to remain in the employ of the school, able to come and go as he pleased when his work was done.

So there was hope here, even in this place. And he embraced the one word that was its highest expectation, seized it and placed it in that innermost secret place alongside the tiny bright flame that had carried him through so many dark places of pain and fear and sorrow.

XII

Inside the cave of refuge, preparations had been made for the midday meal. The men who had been in hiding there were planning to leave as soon as the meal was finished, and they had let down their guard. No sentry stood watch outside. No effort was made to conceal the fire they used for cooking.

As they were about to break bread, they heard the sound of stones being dislodged on the hillside below. Suddenly alert, they paused mid-breath, listening.

Voices, low and indistinct, were climbing the hill toward them.

Zebediah motioned for the others to remain still, then moved to the entrance of the cave, peered out…and nearly fell off the ledge.

What he saw was not the dreaded Romans approaching but rather a single man—not a soldier—accompanied by two females. From the distance he observed them, one of the females looked very much like his sister, Miriam.

For several moments he stood blinking down into the sunlight, doubting his senses. Then the woman who looked like his sister caught sight of him and began to wave her arms vigorously.

"It's Zebediah!" she shouted excitedly, though her companions were no more than arms' length away. "It is! It's Zebediah!" Then, sending her voice up the hill, "Zebediah! It's me, Miriam!"

It was, Miriam! And her daughter, Rachel. No longer a child but a young woman. A beautiful young woman, at that. And the young man with them was his nephew Elihu, the only son of his deceased brother. After Miriam's husband, Jacob, passed away, Eli had moved in with Miriam to help take care of her and her daughter, a responsibility that by custom Zebediah should have been the one to assume.

It required all the patience he could muster, but Zebediah managed to contain his bursting curiosity until they reached the sanctuary of the cave and the visitors were given refreshments before pulling Miriam aside and asking why she had come there—and how she had managed to find him. "I was given a message," she said.

"A message?" Zebediah frowned. "What kind of message?"

"Are you well enough to go about again?" she asked.

The frown deepened. "How did you know about that?"

"The message—"

"What? What are you talking about, Miriam?"

"It…it is all beyond me…" she said, shaking her head.

"Miriam!" In spite of his efforts at self-restraint, the voice of the prophet rose in concert with his arms, which had lifted up and outward in sheer frustration. How could it be, he wondered, that the same sister who as a young girl used to rattle on so ceaselessly could not now put two sentences together in a row and explain what was going on?

"I had a dream," she said at last, her voice low and tentative. In that dream, as she now recounted it, she saw Zebediah standing at the mouth of a hillside cave. He looked aged and gaunt—the cloak draped over one shoulder seemed in danger of sliding off, and his right hand wavered as he raised his staff overhead. But when he spoke, his voice was as strong as ever.

"Come," he said, "the work of the Lord awaits!"

At these words, his disciples gathered about him.

A second time he raised his staff, saying: "Come! You have been called to do the work of the Lord!"

He held his staff forth yet again, and this time when he spoke he called out a single word—the name Rachel.

To her immense surprise, Miriam saw her daughter Rachel emerge from the cluster of disciples and begin to climb the hillside. When she reached the entrance to the cave, she joined hands with Zebediah, and together the two of them stepped off the ledge. But instead of falling, they rose upward. As Miriam watched in wonder, a great arched portal appeared in the sky. Soaring like angels, Rachel and Zebediah ascended to the portal and passed through into the blue-white brilliance beyond.

"Then I heard the voice," she now concluded, "Very soft, like something whispering within me. The voice told me to bring Rachel to you. And then I awoke."

Zebediah was silent, stunned by what he had heard, and even more by what he saw in her eyes. In them he read quite clearly that he was not the only one in the family that the mystery had touched.

"It was a mysterious dream, but still and all a dream," he said, but his voice betrayed more than a hint of uncertainty.

"If you had such a dream, would you not call it a vision?" Miriam asked, not half as much in awe of her brother the prophet as were his followers, or those who came to hear him speak, for she had, after all, grown up with him.

"Well, perhaps, but…"

"Tell me, then," she went on, "does the messenger choose the voice—or does the voice choose the messenger?"

Zebediah threw up his hands in surrender. "Ah, Miriam. Even as a young girl you could always out-talk me. So, how did you find me?"

"I could tell you that I was given directions by the voice in my dream."

"Were you?"

"No," she said, a mischievous smile twinkling briefly in her eyes, making her seem for a moment a young girl again. "The truth is, I remembered that after you had your dream you used to retreat to these hills. You even took me walking with you once. And I recalled that there was a cave that we rested in. A cave that looked out over the valley. You said you often came there to meditate because the view was so peaceful. So I came searching for that cave. In all truth, I was lost until I saw smoke coming from this hill. Perhaps, as you might say, that smoke was a sign from the Lord."

"And what," Zebediah said, "does the messenger tell you now?"

"Nothing," Miriam said flatly. "I heard the voice but once. Oh, I listen, but all I hear is the sound of my own thoughts. I don't know what it all means, Zebediah. I only know what I saw and heard in my dream: that you have not been well, that you are preparing to go out again on your mission, and that somehow Rachel is meant to be with you on your journey. Now I have done as I have been directed. When you are well again, you can return her to me. Until then may the Lord be with you both."

Before Zebediah could utter a word, she went over to Rachel and embraced her. Then, taking her daughter's hands, she placed them in those of her brother. And before the dam of tears could burst, she turned to leave, with only her nephew for a companion.

The great prophet was again caught off guard.

"Wait!" he cried. "You're not leaving? Not so soon. Please…you just got here. Rest awhile. We need to talk…"

But Miriam was already disappearing through the entrance to the cave.

Zebediah looked beseechingly at his followers, but they were standing open-mouthed, apparently even more dumbfounded than he was.

"Wait!" he cried again, hurrying to the mouth of the cave. "Miriam! Eli! Wait! How long is the girl to remain with me?"

The question echoed about the cave without an answer, for Miriam was already beginning to descend the hill, hurrying away not from her daughter or her brother but from something she did not understand.

Throwing his hands in the air again, the prophet scurried a few yards down the incline, pleading with his sister to return. Or at least to answer. But her back kept getting smaller and smaller.

At last he let his hands drop down to his sides. Turning about, he saw the girl, Rachel, standing at the entrance to the cave, trembling, and with wide eyes. Chastising himself for being so thoughtless, he went to her and held out his arms.

"Do not worry, Rachel," he said softly. "All will be well. You will be safe with us. We will go on a brief journey, and then I will return you to the house of your mother. Meanwhile, I want you to know that your presence is a blessing to me."

XIII

Though Lucius Portius had a luxurious private bath in his sprawling townhouse in Rome, he frequented one of the public baths nearly every day to socialize, catch up on gossip, and conduct business and political affairs.

This day he arrived earlier than usual, accompanied by a trusted slave. Leaving the slave to watch over his clothes, he went from the dressing room to the gymnasium to limber up a bit. He worked up a light sweat, then headed for the tepidarium, a warm room with a lukewarm bathing pool. After a brief dip in the pool he paid a visit to a masseur for a massage followed by a scraping with a strigil, the small, curved metal tool used to get rid of sweat, oil, and dead skin.

Next he proceeded on thick soled sandals to protect his feet from the hot tiles of the floor to the caladarium, a warm, steamy room with a hot bath. A few minutes in the caldarium and he went back to the tepidarium to recover from the steam bath before moving on to the frigidarium for a quick, cold plunge which he used both as a physical discipline and to invigorate himself for meeting to come.

Finally he returned to the dressing room to put on his undergarments, toga, and sandals before retreating to a private room overlooking a garden. He had cakes and wine sent in.

As he waited, he reflected that at times he almost wished he had not set up such an efficient intelligence network. As of late the news that filtered back to him from the various corners of the Empire was invariably troublesome, even from outposts like Palestine, where it was rumored that the old troublemaker Zebediah was beginning his activities again. While this particular bit of information was not especially disturbing to Portius (though he recognized that a man who wielded sharp words could be more dangerous than one who wielded a sharp sword), it did help him arrive at the answer to an impending decision that had been vexing him for some time.

Thus, when Justinian Flavius arrived, Lucius Portius was completely prepared.

Flavius entered the room with a broad smile meant to mask his discomfort. It had been some time since the unfortunate incident at the Portius villa at Alba Longa, and while his host had effectively suppressed word of what had occurred, it was still a memory that he found personally mortifying. Not so much the death of the young slave wench as the fact that she apparently preferred to die rather than couple with him. "Ah, General, it is a pleasure to see you again," he said. "You are looking fit, as always."

"And it appears that life in Rome is agreeing with you, Tribune," Portius replied, noting that the younger man had gained a few pounds. "Please…" He waved a hand at the chair opposite him and the tray of cakes and wine. "I took the liberty of ordering some refreshments."

Flavius sat and poured a glass of wine, holding his tongue with some difficulty to keep from inquiring about the occasion for this invitation.

Portius did not keep him waiting long. "One reason I wanted to meet with you, other than that it has been too long since I've enjoyed your company, is to ask if you by chance have heard the latest from your old outpost of Palestine."

"Ah, I'm afraid I've been so involved with matters here, with the Guard, that is, that at times news of the provinces slips by me."

"I see. Well, something has come to my attention that I should apprise you of. It seems that the rabble-rouser who goes by the name of Zebediah was not disposed of after all. In fact, I understand that even now he is going about the countryside, stirring up the people again."

Flavius raised an eyebrow, obviously surprised at the news.

"The reason I brought this up," Portius went on, "is that such reports of unfinished business may not bode well for the advancement of your career. So, I have come up with a remedy that will afford you opportunity to take care of this unfinished business and smooth the path to the success of your future aspirations, much as I spoke about back at my villa."

"That is very…considerate of you. What do you have in mind?"

"My thought was that I could have you appointed to the position of intelligence tribune for the Tenth Legion garrisoned at Caesarea. Such a position would allow you to track the movements of Zebediah and put an end to his mischief. Achieving this would bring you back to Rome in triumph and open any number of doors for you."

Flavius sat there for several moments without replying, full realizing that what was being proposed was not a suggestion; it had already been decided.

"You may recall from our conversation at Alba Longa," Portius went on, "that I wished for my son to gather experience in the military, and that I hoped you might take him under your wing, perhaps as your personal aide. The arrangement, as well as your tenure in Palestine, will be but for a short term. And I can assure you that, from your standpoint, it will time well spent."

"It would be an honor and a privilege to assist in any way I can," Flavius said, managing the words with only the slightest catch in his voice. When the meeting was concluded, Portius stayed there awhile longer, finishing off the wine while he considered how best to break the news to Marcellus Servianus and Claudia. It was a move certain to arouse the displeasure of both of them, especially Marcellus, who would no doubt express extreme resentment at being sent off to Judea. Nevertheless, having his son there would provide a valuable inside view of conditions in the Eastern provinces, an area of vital importance not only to the Empire but also to the fortunes of his family and his son.

Not that it would make any difference to Marcellus. He was not yet able to appreciate the intricacies and thrust of such planning any more than he could appreciate how difficult it was to be a good father—a father willing to displease his offspring for the moment in order to provide maximum benefit in the future.

So Marcellus must be guided still. There were worse places by far than Caesarea, which was actually a splendid seaside city. As well, Palestine would be a safe enough outpost. The people there were given to unreasonable temperament and even occasional revolt, but rarely to military prowess. Moreover, the region was ripe with opportunity, for should certain rumored insurrections have basis in fact, then in due time Marcellus Servianus might very well be in a position to command the force that would crush them. An easy enough task, but one that could well bring him home as a conquering hero. And, of course, add to the luster of the Portius family name.

XIV

An emissary from a Roman senator arrived in Capua to reserve the arena for a private showing. Two pairs were requested. The type of fighting—be it dagger, sword and shield, net and trident, or even some novel combination—did not particularly matter. But the senator did have one stipulation: the second match had to be to the death.

Antonius Cappio voiced his customary protests, concluding with mention of the sum that must be paid if a death match was insisted upon, but it seemed that money was of little consequence.

After the deposit had been paid, Cappio made one half of the death-match choice. The selection of an opponent for Steppan was left up to Braccus.

The young gladiator had passed through each phase of training with remarkably consistent excellence, and had engaged in duels with a variety of wooden and blunted weapons until he was at last judged ready to be matched for points with weapons of steel.

Point matches were by definition contests to a decision, not death, but anything that took place in the arena could be deadly. Thus, when Steppan emerged in each of his first three matches not only victorious but also virtually unscathed, he further bolstered Cappio's opinion that he had purchased a jewel in the rough. The youth was exceptionally quick and agile, and he had strength far beyond his years. Moreover, he walked onto the arena floor without being whipped or prodded.

And there was something else, something smoldering just below the surface that was beyond strength or skill or courage. If that unnamed something could be unleashed, it would make the young barbarian not only a truly superior fighter, but also an invincible one—a gladiator who would bring great riches and glory to the establishment at Capua.

Even such a potentially valuable investment must necessarily be tested, however. And though Antonius Cappio harbored a strong distaste for matches to the death, much preferring point matches—which allowed for an entertaining display of skill and courage, and even a nice flow of blood without unnecessary, and costly, slaughter—he arranged the only true test there was. They were not told until the night before. It was Antonius Cappio's theory that any more notice was undesirable. The daily existence of the gladiators was a constant reminder of their destiny, but it was an existence that most of them could become at least somewhat conditioned to. Only the most unusual of men, however, could endure for any length of time the absolute certainty that on a given day and time he would enter the arena to fight to the death. Even a few days of living with such knowledge affected a man's mind. And his mind affected his body. So they were only told the night before.

Those who wished it were given a woman. Some men thought that lying with a woman would weaken them. Some were so wrapped up in blankets of terror and dread that they could not even think of the act of sex. Others coveted a female, lusted after that rare moment of pleasure in their otherwise miserable lives. Still others wanted a woman for a different kind of comfort—someone to talk to, to cling to, to simply be with on what might be their last night on earth.

Steppan chose to be with a woman. Like many of the slave girls at the school, she was quiet. And afraid. But he, too, was acquainted with torment and humiliation. He, too, was a slave. So he talked to her—asked what she was called and where she was from and how she had come to be in this most dreadful of places. And as the night wore on he touched her, but gently in spite of his growing desire. He whispered to her softly, almost as he had to the horses he had been given to care for, as he caressed the soft curves of her body. And in the end he used her, but in using gave something of himself in return.

Tender in age herself, not much older than this latest one she had been sent to, she felt an unaccustomed flow of emotions for this youthful gladiator. As it happened then, a measure of mercy was granted each of them: they lost something of themselves in one another, if only for a little while. And afterward they slept.

When he awoke, the lightless cell was cold. Tugging at the thin blanket, he covered them both without waking the girl, then lay and looked up at the shadowed ceiling, trying to keep his heartbeat from racing out into the morning. At breakfast the four who were to go into the arena ate apart from the others. By then they knew how they would be paired. Steppan's opponent was to be a Jew, a young man perhaps three or four years older than himself, slight but with a wiry strength and deceptive quickness. The Jew had fought to the death once before, a fact of which Steppan was well aware. Studying him with quick, furtive glances, Steppan noted the strained and brittle look on his face and tried to hide his own anxious dread.

Though he tried with all his might not to think about what lay ahead, Steppan could not help wondering what weapons they would be given. The Jew was quick, and well skilled with the sica—the curved knife honed to razor sharpness for the arena. If they went that route, his own superior strength would be less an advantage. Still, he told himself, in training he was more than a match for anyone in speed and skill.

On the other hand, if they were given the sword and shield, then he would definitely have the advantage. When he found himself dwelling on this latter possibility, building it into hope, he abruptly dismissed it. This, more than any other, was the time for no thought.

Throughout the meal the four spoke scarcely a word. Neither did they eat much, except for Steppan, who ate everything placed before him, chewing slowly without tasting, shoving strength into his body because he would need it.

Though the other gladiators in the dining hall pretended not to pay any special attention to the table of the condemned, from time to time one of them would let his glance linger in that direction. Some of the gladiators were hardened criminals, more than one had been a killer even before coming to this place. Yet if any of them were so lifeless inside that they could not feel a spark of compassion for those who were about to walk onto the sands of death, they could at least hear the distant tolling of the bell of their own hour, and so even they accorded the four the courtesy of silence.

After breakfast the four were seated on narrow wooden benches in the house of expectation—a little stone shed with wooden doors that led onto the arena floor. From outside there came the sounds of laughter and of women's voices, high-pitched and gay and brimming with excitement. Sounds from a far-distant world.

After a while they heard music and knew the dancing girl was about to make her entrance, and with it one of the four began to curse, then moan, and finally he broke down completely and began to weep.

"Stop it!" the one who was to be his opponent hissed, wanting to quiet him before the trainers heard and came to punish them all.

The weeping increased in volume.

"Stop it!" the other man hissed again. "We are not the ones who will die today!" he blurted, unmindful of Steppan and the Jew.

At this the unfortunate wretch lifted his watery eyes and shook his head. "Each time we come here we die," he rasped. "Even when we come away with our lives, a part of us dies. It would be better to end it all at once," he concluded, and the three who sat with him knew that the Romans would see more death this day than they had bargained for.

A trumpet blared, and in the wake of its blast, armed trainers came to extract the first pair. The hysterical one seemed calm then, as if he was resigned to what must happen. He arose on command and marched without prodding to the door. There he turned. "Better to end it all at once!" he declared. And then he began to laugh, a high, shrill, mirthless sound even more terrible than his weeping.

Then the door was shut and bolted, and the next few minutes were lost in a jumbled confusion of noises: a mixture of shrieking and yelling and cajoling voices from the stands punctuated by brief periods of hush fraught with expectation; the sharp clang of blade striking blade; grunts and curses; breathing heavy and labored and laced with fear; a sudden empty moment, quick and prolonged...a scream, isolated and terrible.

Silence.

Then, applause. An obscene sound of clapping hands to signify approval. The trumpet sounded again, and the door to the shed was reopened. The moment from which there was no return came rushing across the hot white sand and around the dark silhouette of the trainers, and a colorless Steppan rose unsteadily to his feet, feeling as if he was about to lose the breakfast he had eaten a short time before. The body that had been so well trained seemed to be failing him; his legs moved independently of command, his eyes did not focus, and his breath came in shallow, labored, gasps.

Steppan and his opponent were led before those who had purchased their shame and terror—seven Roman nobles, three women and four men sitting on cushioned benches of stone attended by slaves who fanned away the heat and flies and served wine in silver goblets and sweet delicacies on jewel-encrusted trays—to give the gladiator's salute, and then Braccus presented them with their weapons.

It was to be sword and shield versus sword and shield, but at that moment it no longer mattered to Steppan. The weapons seemed heavy and unfamiliar in his hands; the shield dangled loosely at his side, and the sword threatened to slip from the grasp of his sweat-dampened palm. He thought he had prepared himself to face death boldly, but now—on this unbearably bright morning of truth—he found himself trembling before a vast, illimitable void, a bottomless pit of darkness from which there was no return.

Braccus lifted the whistle he wore on a cord about his neck and gave the signal for the gladiators to salute one another, and at that instant something that had been with Steppan since before the night of his birth—the same something that Antonius Cappio had sensed without being able to define—broke the bonds that held it and came raging from the dark place of its hiding.

With the second blast of the whistle that signified the contest was to begin a most amazing thing occurred: Steppan turned completely away from his opponent and closed his eyes, presenting his back blindly to the other man's sword.

Though it occupied a mere matter of seconds, the act was so astonishing that it seemed to hold time in abeyance. The whistle dropped from Bracchus's opened lips and dangled before his chest…a horrified Antonius Cappio visualized the blood of his prized investment about to go spilling out over the sand…the audience thought with angry disbelief that the larger fighter was committing suicide, robbing them of their entertainment by taking the coward's way out…and the wiry Jewish gladiator leaped forward, his sword uplifted.

A hoarse, unearthly cry shattered the breathless moment.

In the wake of its sound, Steppan whirled about, but the face that confronted his opponent was not the same one that had been there only moments before—it was a grotesque contortion, a snarling, red-eyed demon's mask of fury.

The beast within had been loosened.

So shocking was the transformation, so frightful the combination of otherworldly sight and otherworldly sound, that the Jewish gladiator nearly dropped his sword. Instead of slashing through Steppan's neck, the blade fell weakly across his chest.

Rejoicing in the stinging flow of its own blood, the beast circled about, a low, brutish growl issuing from its lips. Then it suddenly sprang forward in a furious and blinding attack, the shield a battering ram of irresistible force, pounding an opening for the terrible thrusting, chopping, hacking, slicing sword.

It was such a savage and unconditional assault that it hypnotized spectators, trainers, guards, and even Antonius Cappio, and left the dazed and overwhelmed fighter flat on his back, blood from wounds in his chest and abdomen running together to form a smear of darkened red, one thigh opened and quivering, the hand that had grasped the sword now empty and powerless. The seven Romans looked on in disparate states of wonder, awed on the one hand by the incredible display of ferocity they had witnessed yet disappointed on the other at how quickly the spectacle had ended. And yet, each of them would have readily agreed that what they had viewed had been precisely that: a spectacle, something at once terrifying yet seductively fascinating and beyond the scope of anything they had ever experienced.

Straddling his vanquished opponent, his arms trembling with the effort of restraint, Steppan awaited the verdict.

Carefully avoiding so much as a sideways glance at his companions or at Antonius Cappio, the senator who had convened the party let the decision hang in the balance, extracting the full measure of drama the moment afforded. Raising his right hand in a studied and deliberate manner, he let it hang above his head…then abruptly turned his thumb down toward the ground.

A deep guttural cry rose up from the innermost depths of the beast, and as it erupted in a red-eyed howl of triumph, Steppan gripped the sword with both hands and brought it plunging downward, driving the point of the blade all the way through the chest of his victim and into the sand below.

XV

The only problem now was how best to use him. If handled properly, he could be a walking gold mine, as much in demand as any gladiator in all the empire. Throughout the years Antonius Cappio had seen some splendid fighting machines: men so startlingly quick they could snake in and out and deliver a fatal blow before the eye could warn the brain; great, sinewy men of such awesome and unrelenting strength that they defied all attack and robbed opponents of their courage just before they robbed them of their lives; men possessed of a special type of cunning that enabled them to assess other men's strengths and turn them into weaknesses; still other men with the great heart of a lion, rare individuals who looked fear in the eye and made it an ally, who triumphed because they would not admit defeat.

But never in all his experience had Cappio beheld in one single fighter such a combination of lightning-bolt quickness and colossal power, of inborn skills and almost mindless courage, as he saw in the young barbarian.

There was something else about this one as well, a bonus that would further enhance his value. His handsome features held an unquestionable appeal for the ladies. Cappio had taken care to observe the reaction of female spectators. And when Steppan was brought forth, his muscular physique highlighted with oil, the ladies confirmed by their unwavering stares and slightly parted lips what Cappio had suspected.

So all the talent was there, and in abundance, yet it had to be put to the proper use. It was essential that he be assigned a specialty, one primary method of fighting into which he could channel all his energies, for only in that manner could he maximize his chances for continued success—and therefore continued survival. Normally this was not a particularly difficult decision for Cappio and his trainers to make, but Steppan presented a most unusual situation.

Steppan was, for example, an outstanding archer. At one time, bowmen were commonly sent into the arena against wild animals, but as the crowds became more sophisticated, and thus more bloodthirsty, such contests between men and beast fell from popularity. For one thing, the beast almost always lost to the bow and arrow. Now in order to arouse a crowd, a man had to be sent out against a lion or tiger with only a dagger in his hands—which drastically altered the odds in the other direction. Though Cappio easily dismissed the thought of using the young barbarian as an archer, he could not help but speculate how Steppan and a dagger might fare against a wild beast.

As a retiarri, a wielder of net and trident, Steppan was least suited. He had the quickness to spread the net and the strength to wield the long handled fork, but he was at times short on the patience required for their maximum use. More important, as far as Cappio was concerned, the net and trident was far less popular with the masses than sword or dagger play.

The real decision, then, lay between the sword and shield and the dagger. Steppan's superb combination of power and speed and endurance rendered him virtually matchless with the sword and shield, but in some respects he was equally as good with the sica, the long, curved dagger shaped somewhat like the tusk of a wild boar.

The Thracians and Jews most often excelled with the sica. And they were usually smaller men, lithe and swift, able to dart in and out with such fierce celerity that the spectator dared not glance away for fear of missing the decisive thrust. Thracian play, as such contests were commonly referred to, had become the most popular of all gladiatorial events, flashing and deadly and intensely exciting to watch, and it was therefore only natural that Cappio would strongly consider this specialty for Steppan.

The barbarian appeared overly large and muscular to excel with the knife, but he was second to none in speed and agility, and he had an unmatched ability to feint and elude, to select the proper opening at the proper moment.

Not long after the death match against the Jew, Cappio had tested Steppan with the sica against a man from another school, and Steppan had emerged victorious again, walking away with only a thin ribbon of blood across one thigh.

In due time Cappio had sent him back to the hard-packed sand with the sword and shield, and yet again with the curved dagger, testing, judging, comparing—and anxiously so, for he had become acutely aware of how valuable Steppan had become.

With the sword, Cappio's prized fighter was pitted against a huge German in a breathtaking match of howling, clashing fury that ended with a red-eyed raging beast straddling a nearly decapitated Teutonic corpse.

With the dagger Steppan had granted his opponent early retirement from the ranks of fighting men, sweeping behind him to slice through the hamstring of a thigh.

So there was an important decision to be made, and it was anything but easy. As things now stood, Cappio leaned toward the sword and shield. Here Steppan was not only ideally suited but to some degree less likely to suffer one of the untimely but non-fatal wounds—the sliced hamstring, the severed tendon, the gouged-out eye—that plagued the wielders of the sica and cut short so many careers. All arena play was deadly, but none so capricious as Thracian play. But then, as an expert in such fighting, Steppan would be in great demand, and thus would bring even more silver into the coffers of the school.

And so the debate wound back upon itself.

Meanwhile, Antonius Cappio made every effort to bring the centerpiece of his stable along with the utmost care, personally supervising his training and his diet, matching him prudently and with caution, building up his powers, his confidence, his reputation…and his value.

XVI

The members of the little band made their way slowly, unaware that eyes were watching from afar. There were five of them: Zebediah, Jarel, two followers who had survived the massacre at the Jordan and afterward abided in the cave of hiding, and Rachel. Day after day they trudged on, Zebediah limping along in the lead, following no directions other than those of the voice within. When they came to the town of Hebron the voice spoke strongly to Zebediah, so he paused there to deliver his message. As had happened before, people found his words to be good and true, and when he resumed his journey, his words went out before him.

But there were other words that preceded him as well, words that were neither good nor true. To some it was a source of scandal that a young woman should be traveling about with four men, and since gossip and ugly rumors tend to spread swifter and wider than words of peace and joy, lewd insinuations followed the group wherever they went. Men, inflamed by Rachel's striking beauty, easily imagined her performing services of the basest nature for her male companions. Women, jealous of the manner in which the eyes of their men fastened upon the girl, made no effort to defend her.

In places all along their route, Rachel heard vile and terrible words whispered as she passed by. And even when she did not hear such words, she felt them in the dark-hooded depths of watching eyes. Hurt and bewildered, and saddened to think that because of her presence the message of Zebediah might fall on deaf ears, she retreated within herself, hoping that she would not be noticed, hoping that she would not put herself, or the others, in jeopardy.

The hope, though noble, was not easily realized. Two days' journey from Hebron, as they approached a village near the shore of the Dead Sea, a combination of tired feet and wandering mind caused Rachel to fall behind the others.

Suddenly two men blocked her path.

"Are you traveling with that preacher and his men?" one of them said.

Rachel halted, startled by the intrusion. "Yes," she answered, only then realizing that she had become separated from her companions.

"How lucky for them," the other man said, letting his gaze sweep over her in a slow, insolent manner that left no doubt as to his meaning.

"So, which of them is your husband?" the first one asked.

"I…I have no husband."

"No husband? Tell me, then, do you perform the wifely duty for all of them?" he said, a wicked grin twisting his features. "If so, we'll gladly join your little band."

Rachel's face reddened. She tried to step around the two, but one of them grabbed her arm.

"Take your hands off my sister!" a voice demanded.

A sturdy-looking young man grasping an even sturdier-looking staff came striding into view.

The two would-be abductors looked at one another and quickly released the girl.

"She's your sister?" one of them said. "We…we didn't know…"

Jarel's eyes narrowed. "You didn't know!" He took a step forward. "And so you thought that excused your actions!"

"I…we…" the two broke and ran like the cowards they were.

Rachel watched them go with a surge of relief that left her weak in the knees.

"Your sister?" she said, smiling up at Jarel as they hurried to catch up with the others.

"We are all brothers and sisters of the Lord," he replied. Something in his eyes said, or at least so she interpreted, that in other times and circumstances he just might not look on her exactly as a sister.

That night Zebediah and his disciples were guests for the night in the home of a local man who had known the prophet before the incident on the Jordan River.

When the evening meal was finished, Rachel went outside, apart from the others. Settling down beneath a tree, she began to comb her hair. Someday, she thought, smiling, taking absent-minded delight in the long, clean pull of the comb, she would like to settle down in a place of her own. A home, with a husband and children. She did not imagine her house as being overly large or elaborate. In fact, she did not visualize any of it clearly at all—especially the part of the husband. Instead she harbored two vague images: one of masculine strength and beauty and tenderness and the other of undefined walls enclosing light and love and laughter. She would look after husband and home and children with love and care. Her family and her home would be an extension of herself, and she would be happy for the rest of her days.

It did not seem too much to ask, and now she prayed that it was not, that it would someday all come to pass—and in the not-too-distant future, for she was not getting any younger.

Finished with her hair, she put the comb aside and let her thoughts drift to the vast, star-sprinkled sky. When she had been a little girl, her mother had told her that each star was an angel. Much more recently, a man they had encountered during their travels told of a great library with scrolls on which it was written that the universe was filled with a number of suns, great heavenly bodies not seen during the day but visible at night as the tiny lights men call stars. Could that be? she marveled. Other suns in the heavens? If so, there might be other worlds as well. And if there were other worlds, there might be other people.

It was all very confusing. The prophets and the wise men told that one God created one heaven and one earth. One, that was all. Anything more was not spoken of, and that much alone was far beyond understanding. Just as were all the questions, the longings, the many things unknown, both seen and unseen. Zebediah had once said that Why is a mystery.

And so, she thought, are What and When.

Suddenly very sleepy, she arose and quietly made her way inside to the pallet where she would spend the night. Too young then to be greatly troubled by questions on the nature of the universe, she stretched out and almost immediately fell asleep.

XVII

It took several weeks for the first message to travel from Caesarea to Rome. "Greetings to Lucius Cornelius Portius, noble and most esteemed General and Senator," it began, prompting the named recipient to snort impatiently at the excess of words.

"I am highly pleased," the missive went on, "to be able to report with favor on the progress of your son, Marcellus Servianus. He seems to have adjusted admirably well to life as it must be lived on the frontier. Not only does his military prowess grow from day to day, but he displays clearly defined qualities of leadership. In short, the youth you were so gravely concerned about is rapidly becoming a man and a soldier."

Lucius Portius finished the letter with another disdainful snort. The report that Justinian Flavius sent was little more than an obvious attempt to curry favor, but that was to be expected. What really mattered was that the basic purpose was apparently being accomplished, the groundwork firmly laid.

Subsequent messages arrived at regular intervals, but while they were unfailingly encouraging concerning the progress of Marcellus Servianus, they contained an annoying paucity of hard information about political affairs. The only thing of note that Flavius had to report was that certain Jewish religious fanatics were stirring up the population again. But, the intelligence tribune added, that was of little concern to Rome because such troublemakers seemed unpopular even with the majority of their own people.

Letters from Marcellus Servianus were fewer and farther apart. Still chafing at having been banished from civilization, he had decided to punish his father and mother alike (for surely she could have done something to change his father's mind, could have somehow prevented his being sent halfway across the world to this barbaric place) by maintaining a distant silence. Such resolve soon faltered, however. Marcellus accumulated experiences, became in his own eyes something of a man of the world. Before long it seemed more important to let his parents, in particular his father, know how much he had grown than it was to maintain a code of silence. Thus he wrote:

"It is a strange land to which I have come. The heat can be utterly stifling, the food outside the garrison is suspect and at times quite disgusting, and the natives of the region are anything but to be trusted. On the other hand, the city commands an excellent view of the harbor, and our garrison, with its familiarity of language and customs, serves as an extension of our homeland, especially for those of the lower classes. All of which is not to say that there is much in the way of comfort here, for there is precious little of that, although there is a gymnasium with a decent bath. And, though I have not yet viewed it firsthand, I have heard rumors of the existence of a small arena nearby. Supposedly, such a structure would be an affront to the people here, though I cannot imagine why this would be so, or why it should be of any concern to us. After all, we are here as conquerors, not as visitors."

The second message from Marcellus Servianus brought word of his impending first campaign. "The religious zealots are becoming ever more bold. Flavius seems increasingly concerned about the one called Zebediah. It is his opinion that unless we make a show of force against this man, his followers will grow in strength to the point of armed aggression. Obviously such an occurrence cannot be permitted. Thus, by the time you read this, a detachment of our Legion will have marched toward Lake Tiberius with the objective of seeking out this Zebediah and his group of fanatics. I am proud to report that not only will I be among those taking part in such a campaign, but moreover I will be at the right hand of Flavius as his next-in-command."

Marcellus Servianus signed off with the request that his parents pray to the gods for the success of his mission.

XVIII

It had been a stroke of genius. Sheer genius. Of course, he had recognized that within himself for some time. But now, as he was borne along the streets of Rome by six sturdy litter bearers, he could see verification of his genius amply displayed everywhere about him. On carefully lettered placards, in uneven graffiti scrawled on the sides of buildings and walls, and from the babbling lips of the horde of people scurrying to the arena, the single and ultimate symbol of confirmation of his brainchild was repeated over and over again: Cestus...Cestus...Cestus!

The word was simple enough in itself, until recent times denoting the leather hand covering worn by boxers in the arena. Because it was an unarmed style of combat, boxing had fallen so far down the list of popularity as to become obsolete. But then, in the course of his unceasing quest for some new twist to add spice and variety to arena play, something to capture anew the fancy of the crowd, Antonius Cappio had stumbled onto the idea of attaching sharp-pointed spikes to the knuckles of the gloves, thereby making them potentially lethal.

Still, the new device held very little promise of appeal to the masses. Not, that is, until Cappio's second inspiration. Sitting alone late one night with a goblet of wine for company, he conceived the unlikely idea of matching a man equipped only with spiked gloves against a man armed with sword and shield or sica.

Experiments at Capua proved such matches to be less one-sided than expected. A fighter of superior skill and speed could avoid the relatively heavy movements of the sword, and even deflect and block with steel-tipped hands the quick slices and thrusts of the dagger, then close in and drive penetrating blows to the abdomen or kidneys or kill more quickly by piercing the eyes or throat or brain. So a few select men were trained in the art of the cestus, and in time matched against armed opponents.

This newest form of arena play became an instant success. As anticipated, the knife or sword would most often prevail, and the boxer would die in a run of blood terrible enough to satisfy the most morbid public taste. But there were times when the relatively unarmed fighter would triumph, would somehow avoid the seemingly unavoidable and dart in for the kill. Amazed and enraptured, the crowd would see the armed man fall, blood spurting from deep and fatal wounds, hard sharp steel vanquished by fists and skill and courage.

Such novel spectacles provided not only ample bloodshed, but a new dimension of drama as well, and in so doing created a new breed of arena champion. For when the virtually unarmed fighter did conquer the odds and emerge victorious, he became something of a celebrated hero, a gladiator worthy of the highest praise and laurels.

Naturally it was not long before other schools began training men in the way of the spiked cestus. But of the few men who practiced this unique form of combat, none was so accomplished as the gladiator Steppan from the school of Antonius Cappio. At once as strong as the bulls and as quick as the jungle cats that sometimes occupied the arena before him, he could avoid the sweep of the sword or the slashing blade of the knife and then spring in to bring his opponent down, often with a single, terrible, triumphant blow. Time after time he went striding onto the sand, raised his fist in salute, then battered the life out of the one who had come there to kill him.

Men traveled from the far distant points of the Empire to marvel at this new fighter's prowess. Women flocked to the arena to gaze admiringly upon his person, and boys young and old emulated his movements in their own bloodless games. A fighter without parallel, he brought unprecedented heights of money and fame to his owner and was granted certain rewards in return. He was fed the best food, and he was given a monetary award for each victory and allowed to keep the coins that were showered into the arena after each of his appearances. He was proffered not only the company of the most attractive women the school had to offer but the attention of some ladies who lived far outside its confines as well, for there were any number of female admirers of the famed gladiator who were most anxious to display the full extent of their admiration—and influential enough to arrange such a display.

So overwhelming was his power, so notorious his acclaim, that in time he came to be known not by the name given him at birth but by that of the singular instrument of death he wore: the cestus.

Now the man who created this god of the arena pulled shut the curtains of his litter and leaned back to contemplate the recent train of events leading to the arena where the richest match in the history of the Games was about to take place—a match that would, one way or the other, end the illustrious career of the most famous fighter in the world.

Just before leaving for Rome, Antonius Cappio had summoned that fighter up to his villa in Capua. It was an extraordinary act, for never before had one of Cappio's gladiators set foot in his house. Even Braccus had only been allowed there after he had become a freedman.

When Cestus was brought before him, Cappio waited nearly a full minute before speaking, looking out at the carefully tended garden of shrubs and flowers in the courtyard as if even yet weighing the decision. "I remember well the day you first passed through these gates," he said at last. "In that time you have grown from a mere youth to a true gladiator. The best of the best."

Cestus seemed as oblivious to the words of praise as he was to the marble and gold lavishness of his surroundings. Stoic and impassive as ever, he looked straight ahead, waiting for whatever might come.

"As you know," Cappio went on, "I take the best care of my fighters. I give them the finest training, the most nourishing food, warm clothing, baths, massage...even women."

Still there was no response. No sound, no movement, no discernable flicker of emotion. Despite the presence of both his personal bodyguard and Braccus, Cappio was beginning to regret his decision to bring this creature into his house. Outside of the arena, Cestus was normally not given to violence. Indeed, according to Braccus, he was so quiet and mild-mannered that the man and the gladiator seemed to be two separate beings. Yet time and time again, Cappio had witnessed the sudden and startling transformation that summoned the beast from its dark and hidden place. Now he could not help but wonder how closely the demon lurked behind those unreadable eyes. "I do these things not because I must," he continued, bringing his mind back to the matter at hand, "but of my own free will. And so I have brought you here today. Because I like to think of myself as a just man, a fair man, I believe in reward for effort. Your skill has helped my enterprise here flourish all the more, and so it is only fitting that you be rewarded. And what greater reward could I offer…than the gift of freedom?"

At last there was a reaction. For the briefest of moments, Cestus dared to fix his owner with a direct and probing stare.

"Yes," Cappio affirmed, his lips forming into a thin smile. "Your ears serve you well. Three days hence you will fight in the arena at Rome. Win this match, Cestus, and you walk away a free man. Free. Forever."

Though his mouth opened, Cestus still did not speak. Unable to give voice to the questions whirling within him, he retreated into the harbor of no-thought so that he would not do the one thing he truly wished to do.

"Braccus will give you the details," Cappio concluded, glad to have the matter said and done.

Cestus stiffened and gave the gladiator's formal salute, his right fist tightly clenched to his chest. Then he turned and followed Braccus back to the barracks, still not having uttered a single word.

When he was alone again, Antonius Cappio poured a cup of wine and drained it in a single gulp, then sat staring into the depths of the empty vessel, considering what he had done.

Some days before, he had entertained visitors from Rome, among them Paulus Lucinus, commander of the Praetorian Guard. During the course of a series of matches, and a series of flasks of wine, Paulus and several other members of the party from Rome had loudly asserted that the very best of gladiators—who were, after all, nothing more than slaves—would be no match for even an ordinary Roman soldier. Cappio did his best to smile and hold his tongue, but when such remarks not only continued but were obviously—and quite rudely—pointed in his direction, his volatile nature overrode his better judgment.

There was a simple way to decide such a matter, Cappio declared. He would match one of his gladiators against any legionary the gentlemen from Rome cared to produce. Moreover, the gladiator would be armed with only the cestus while the soldier of Rome could have his pick of weapons and armor. Furthermore, he concluded, his flaring temper having taken control of his tongue, he would back his position with half a million sesterces.

Temporarily taken aback, the members of the Roman party held a quick caucus, and then, with little choice if they were to save face, agreed. Smilingly so, for the champion they proposed was none other than the legendary Titus, a soldier of immense size and reputation and a member of the Emperor's personal bodyguard. The Romans, all of them men of financial means, personally guaranteed the amount of the purse, though Paulus Lucinus declared with a smirk that "it might well be that Tiberius himself will wish to handle that end of the arrangement. Especially since there will be absolutely no danger to the Imperial Treasury."

The moment his visitors departed, the mask vanished and Cappio stormed about the villa, cursing the Romans and his own rashness alike. Five hundred thousand sesterces! More than enough to buy a small army of slaves! Even worse, Cestus, the only gladiator he considered not expendable, was his only choice if had any hope of winning the wager—into the arena armed with nothing more than spike tipped gloves while Titus, a giant if ever there was one, a man considered by many to be the most formidable fighter in all the Roman Legion, was to be allowed full weapons and armor!

Pacing furiously about, he ranted and roared and pulled at his thinning hair until the blood pounding in his head threatened to gush forth from his ears. At last, gasping for breath and fearing an attack of apoplexy, he collapsed on a couch, called for a flask of wine, and began to search for ways to control the potential damage to his personal treasury.

His first idea was to secure a position as promoter of the event—a move he calculated would ensure revenues enough to offset a fair portion of the wager if the Roman giant prevailed. Next he took advantage of what would surely be rabid interest in the event to arrange matches that pitted fighters from his school against fighters from other schools at fees considerably below normal, thereby saving not only money but the flesh of his own gladiators as well, flesh that could be put to profitable use on another day.

These things done, Cappio began to regain some of his self-confidence. It was true that Titus was a renowned fighter. On the surface, he appeared to have a clear advantage, but Cestus was at home in the arena. That was his battleground. And though it might seem that Cestus was sentenced to death by his lack of weapons and armor, many eyes had witnessed that same "weaponless" fighter bring an abrupt end to an opponent overly sure of protective steel.

Yet there had to be something more he could do, Cappio fretted. Something to tip the scales in his favor, no matter how slightly. The answer was obvious, nothing more than an acknowledgment of what would happen on that momentous day in the arena: Cestus would live…or Cestus would die.

If Cestus prevailed, Cappio would win a small fortune. If Cestus was vanquished, that same fortune would be handed over to the greedy hands of the nobles from Rome. Either way, Cappio would lose his most glorious fighter, for it was almost certain that should Cestus win, he would be granted freedom by popular acclaim. Thus what Cappio came to offer was nothing more than what would take place in the natural order of things. But by making the gesture himself, he might be able to gain the edge he was searching for. The promise of freedom might be a more powerful weapon than the fear of death.

Now, however, as he approached the shadow of the arena, his confidence began to evaporate. Muttering frantic promises to gods he had never believed in, he hurriedly sought out his head trainer for the latest report.

"All seems well," Braccus said in answer to Cappio's furrowed brow.

"Did he sleep well last night?"

"Yes. But he did ask to be let out in the yard."

"And you granted his wish?"

"Yes. There seemed no harm in it. Of course I remained nearby where I could see him. He stood for some time, just looking up at the sky. Then he said he was ready to sleep."

"And you say he slept?"

"He was asleep when I looked in on him."

"So then, everything seems as usual…"

Braccus gave a slight shrug. "With that one, everything always seems the same," he answered.

"That," Cappio said, "is precisely what I am counting on."

XIX

Things were not the same. Though Cestus tried with all his might, no-thought was not a state to be entered into this day. Ghosts kept flowing out from the past; visions of fire and ashes and screaming death pursued him, caught him, and held him fast; the pounding tension of the moment entered him with his every shallow breath to lodge deep within his bowels. Yet he abided, silent and motionless as a stone, for other than retreating within, there was no place to go.

Three of them waited in the breathless shadows of the house of expectation: one pair and half of another. The fourth, the fabled Titus, was among the entourage ensconced in the podium, the first level of seating in the Coliseum, waiting in comfort until he would be summoned to the arena floor to dispatch of the slave Cestus."

Among the three scarcely a word was spoken. Each man sat in mute communion with himself, waiting in the small enclosure beneath the arena until the agonizing preliminaries of parades and music and dancers and jugglers and archers (preliminaries of color and gaiety and skill, for this was a most festive occasion) followed by point matches had run their course. When at last the trainers came to summon the first pair, they saw that one of the condemned had left his breakfast on the floor.

Then the door was shut and made fast again, leaving Cestus to wait alone. Rising up abruptly, he began to pace from wall to wall, gasping for breath beneath a suffocating blanket of abject and immutable fear. Noises from the crowed, uneven waves of demented cheering and roaring, hammered at the door. Trembling, he hammered in return with fists suddenly impotent. Then his legs gave way, sending him to the floor.

For several long moments he lay there, letting forth a low, mournful wail that encircled the pitiful enclosure and fell heavily back upon its source. In the midst of his anguish, the howling red-eyed demon came rushing from its hidden place. Cestus closed his eyes to look it fully in the face. And when he could see it clearly, he reached out and embraced it.

Seated beside the commander of the Praetorian Guard, with the Emperor Tiberius in the very next box, the mighty Titus reveled in the moment at hand. It seemed to him that all the power and glory of Rome was embodied within those amphitheater walls—and he had been chosen to be its champion. Such a heady thought boosted his already considerable self-confidence to a towering peak. He had seen this Cestus in action, and the gladiator was admittedly a fighter to behold—but not nearly good enough to triumph this day. Particularly when it was to be sword and shield against those puny little gloves.

So confident did Titus become that he even wondered if perhaps the slave had done something to seriously offend his owner. If that was the case, then this lanista named Cappio was a shrewd one, for execution in the arena would be a profitable means of disposal. And it would be profitable to him, as well, Titus thought. He inwardly smiled, envisioning the silver that would soon fill his purse...and the women who would clamor for his favor.

The certitude with which Titus approached the moment was not his alone, for it was inconceivable to most of the privileged Romans sitting nearby that a half-naked barbarian, even one who bore the name Cestus, equipped only with fists encased in spike-tipped gloves would stand the slightest chance against the Emperor's own bodyguard armed with a sword. Indeed, inasmuch as the majority of this class of spectators had made elaborate preparations to enjoy a truly momentous day at the Games, they were mostly concerned that it might all end with disappointing swiftness. When the guards opened the door to the waiting shed the second time, Cestus was ready and waiting. He burst forth from the shadowed place of his transformation with a low, visceral growl and went rushing out onto the hard-packed sand, eager to have it begin.

As he came into view, the crowd roared in recognition. Then spectators began chanting a single word that fused in rhythm and grew in volume until it filled the arena with the throbbing, pulsing drumbeat of Cestus!...Cestus!...Cestus!...Cestus!

Riding the beast now, holding it just under control, Cestus went striding to the center of the arena. He clenched his right hand into a fist and raised it high above his head in a salute to the crowd, a gesture that brought an even louder and more frenzied uproar from the arena seats.

Just when the commotion began to wane, Titus appeared on the arena floor, and the cheering and shouting erupted anew. This time, however, the noise was almost exclusively from the seats of the upper classes, and it was several decibels lower.

The combatants were marched before the Emperor's box to pay homage to Tiberius before being armed by their respective handlers. Titus had made his entrance wearing a breastplate over his uniform, his helmet held formally at his side. Now he carefully fitted the helmet in place, and then held out his hands for his personal sword and shield, openly studying his opponent all the while. The notorious Cestus appeared larger when viewed from up close, and obviously well conditioned—hard of muscle and lean of fat. But, Titus assured himself, even the strongest of sinews parted easily before the sharp steel of a sword.

In contrast, as Cestus held out his hands for Braccus to put in place the gloves from which he took his name, he appeared to merely glance at his opponent. Still, he saw what he needed to see. The Roman was truly huge. Tall and broad and large of bone, but the flesh was loose on his arms. At his waist and back it would be even more so. No doubt this Titus had strength and experience, but his endurance was almost certain to be lacking.

Working swiftly but with the utmost care, Braccus securely fastened the sharp-tipped gloves. He had been in and around the arena for more years than he cared to think about, had known more than his fill of bloodshed, of butchery in the name of sport, yet this was one fight he did not want to miss, one that even he would have paid to witness.

His task completed, Braccus hesitated. He was a free man now, but he had once been a slave, and a gladiator. Quickly, before he had time to think about it and so change his mind, he reached out and clasped Cestus on the shoulder.

"Luck be with you," he blurted, then turned and left the arena floor, hurrying to get to his viewing place before the action began. Titus had witnessed Cestus in the arena firsthand, but nothing he had seen or been told could have fully prepared him for what transpired at the signal to begin. One moment the gladiator was standing stock still, as if he was a unaware of where he was or what was about to transpire, the next he was hurtling through the air with an unearthly shriek issuing from his contorted lips. There was no preliminary measuring, no feinting or probing, just a sudden explosive, leaping, howling rush.

Titus felt his left arm being pulled down with incredible force, saw the flash of spikes coming through the empty space where the shield should have been…

and twisted his head away just in time for the brass of his helmet to deflect the blunt of the blow. Recovering, he brought the hilt of his sword around in a swift arc and used it as a hammer to pound away with quick, defensive chopping movements.

As quickly as he had attacked, Cestus sprang away and began to circle, maintaining his distance. Keeping just out of reach of the sword, his glowing eyes watched for the next opening.

Recovering from the shock of the attack, Titus used his heavy sword and shield to gradually work Cestus ever closer to the wall, narrowing the avenue of escape. When the position was right, he faked a forward lunge, skillfully anticipated Cestus's counter movement, and whirled in that direction. Only because of the quicksilver reflexes of the gladiator did the blade fall short of its target, leaving a thin crimson thread from shoulder to chest instead of a headless torso.

Cestus spun away from the wall, but Titus did not pursue him. Instead, he raised his sword aloft and beckoned Cestus back, then let out a taunting laugh.

By way of reply, the barbarian wiped his right hand slowly across the wound, then lifted a blood-tinged finger to his mouth and licked it clean. Then, with an answering laugh, he sprang back into battle.

Moving in a broken rhythm, feinting here and there, probing, testing, watching, waiting, Cestus wound his gigantic opponent around in an ever-tightening circle. Laboring beneath the heat of the sun and the weight of his armor, Titus tried to reverse directions, felt his feet betray him, saw the arena begin to tilt… and thrust his sword out wildly.

As he tumbled to the arena floor, Titus thought that surely he was dead, but Cestus let out a hiss and dropped to one knee. Scrambling to his feet, Titus saw to his utter amazement that the blade had somehow found the barbarian's thigh.

Before Titus could recover and attack, Cestus pushed himself up and limped back a few paces. Instinct told him the wound was not deep; but it was serious nonetheless, for it would have the effect of slowing his actions. Whatever he was to do, he must do it quickly.

For several moments the two stood measuring one another with unblinking eyes, then Titus let out a bellowing roar and launched a ferocious offensive, thrusting and hacking and slicing with mindless fear and rage, determined to have it over and done.

Always before, the gladiator had met every challenge with an almost joyous fury, but the wound in his thigh had taken away a measure of both his power and his ability to maneuver. Now, for the first time ever, the pride of the arena felt himself becoming the hunted instead of the hunter. Shifting, retreating, avoiding the sword with backward leaps and sideways slips and dodges, he struggled to maintain the gap between himself and his pursuer. He had no strategy, no thought-out plan of battle; his moves were born of a sheer animal instinct for survival. And as the match wore on, the power of the beast seemed to be draining away. Retreating yet again, he went searching deeper within, desperately seeking for a way to avoid the relentless approach of the long-stalking shadow.

Titus was narrowing the circle of sand, edging Cestus ever nearer to the enclosing wall, and almost as one, the crowd members sensed that the end was near. Leaning forward in their seats, the people craned their necks in anticipation. While it had not been a bloody contest thus far, it had nonetheless been truly exciting. More than a match or a contest, it had been an event, a momentous occasion that would be the topic of conversation for months—even years—to come. And having witnessed it this far, no one wanted to miss the conclusion.

For Antonius Cappio, it was too much to bear. Throughout the heart-stopping match, he had found himself cheering for Cestus with unrestricted fervor—not so much because of his wager, or the time and money he had invested in the slave, but simply because he wanted Cestus to win, to somehow emerge victorious in spite of all the odds. Now, as the gladiator retreated before the inexorable advance of the Roman sword, Cappio conceded the futility of his hope, saw clearly the impending end and with it the death as well of something he had long nurtured: the idea that a man could rise above the caste of his birth, could by hard work and careful planning overcome the adversity of unkind fate and stand on equal footing with those more favored from the womb with distinction of class and wealth. For as the cruel spectacle drew to a close, it was painfully evident that the world was exactly the way it had always been: money and the power it spawned would inevitably win out, would triumph over talent, over skill, over courage, even over a desire to prevail so all-consuming that it was the bright flame of life itself.

Cestus had all those things, and yet he was about to die a death that money had purchased. And, he Antonius Cappio, had brains and ability beyond the majority of those who that very day held a seat in the Senate, and yet never would he join their ranks. Never—no matter how great a fortune he might amass—would he escape the class into which he had been born. Thus, for the first time ever during a match, Antonius Cappio closed his eyes to the action, unwilling to witness the death of his lifelong dream.

Uttering a savage oath, Titus lunged forward and swung his sword in a monstrous double arc that aimed first for the head then immediately back down and around, slicing —should the first sweep miss - for the injured leg.

As the sword swept toward his face, Cestus jerked his head back and thrust his arms low and away as he had a thousand times in practice, and then—so quickly that the two movements were one—he sprang forward, leaping high above the momentarily lowered shield.

For one fleeting instant, Cestus looked into the other man's eyes, beheld there unshuttered the startled embryo of shocked disbelief, and then thrust his spiked right fist into Titus's upturned throat. Titus wavered, a silent scream issuing from his narrowed mouth, his sword falling away from his powerless grasp.

Roaring with triumph, Cestus rode Titus to the ground, then tore off the Roman giant's helmet and drove the instrument from which he took his name down one final time.

XX

Though Rachel had seen the phenomenon several times before, she was still amazed. It was almost as if some unseen messenger was telling people when and where Zebediah would appear. The prophet and his little band of disciples had come down out of the hills early that morning. As they made their way into the heat and dust of the valley, they were joined by others, one or two or three at a time, until their ranks had swollen more than tenfold.

When they arrived at the river, they found hundreds more waiting—people of all ages, women and children sprinkled liberally among the men, many of them suffering, crying out for deliverance in voices filled with pain. Though the prophet Zebediah claimed no miracles himself, it was said that on several occasions those who listened to his words had been miraculously healed. And so they came, those troubled in body and mind and spirit, yearning to be set free.

As was customary, the disciples went out among the crowd to minister to the sick and elderly. There were more than ever today, Rachel thought, overwhelmed by sights and sounds and smells of sorrow. She bent down to change a bandage and offer soft words of encouragement to a watery-eyed old woman with skin as dry and wrinkled as the brown distant hills.

"Peace be with you all," Zebediah said. And with this benediction the ragged assembly began to come to order.

"Today I must speak quickly, for my presence is a danger to you," he said. And despite her better instincts, Rachel felt a tinge of annoyance that he had begun to speak while she was yet so far removed from his side. "Even so, I must speak the message that has been given me to deliver. Listen and rejoice, for the time is at hand. Even now the Promised One draws near."

At this an unsteady murmur ran through the crowd, and many of the people began to look searchingly about, taking the words of the prophet at face value.

"Let us prepare ourselves for his coming," Zebediah continued, and the people stilled before his voice. "We all know that we have been oppressed by others for as long as any of us can remember, but I have been sent here today to remind you that what you give out will be given to you in return. Therefore, let us show love to our fellow man and forgive those who have transgressed against us, for it is only through the gates of love that we shall enter into life everlasting."

A man near the front of the crowd frowned and shook his head in protest. "You have only yourself to care for," he called out. "But what of us who have families to tend to? Are we to show love to the Romans when they steal our land and burden us with taxes?"

"It is true that I have no family of my own to tend to, but it is true as well that I have felt the wrath of the Romans firsthand," Zebediah answered. "Yet what could they hope to destroy except this mortal old body? My spirit they could not touch, so long as I did not deliver it up to them myself.

"Consider, my brothers and sisters, what would happen if you took up the sword against the Romans. You might kill a number of them, but others would come to take their place, and in time you, yourself, would be killed, and then your families would suffer all the more. Violence only begets more violence— with this there is no end. Are we to become as Romans, then, in order to free ourselves from Rome?

"You see, we are all brothers and sisters, born of the same Creator. And as long as anyone among us does not live in peace, neither does the greater body. Those who slay the flesh of others slay their own souls. And which of the two is the greater death?"

Even as the question hung between the prophet and his listeners, a distant shout rang out, a single word barked in military fashion. And Zebediah knew without raising his eyes in the direction of the sound that it was the summer of death come to visit again.

In the wake of the sharp command, the Romans came charging down the hill, helmets glistening in the sun, weapons leveled and ready. For several long seconds the people stood rooted in shock and bewilderment, then panic broke out among them. Shouting, screaming, cursing, wailing, they scrambled wildly in all directions.

Rachel, who still remained near the back of the crowd, was momentarily caught up in the frenzy, and then she lost something of herself and sought for the safety of Zebediah. Calling out his name, she tried to move toward him, but the frantic horde turned her around and sent her sprawling on the swift, uneven slope. Beneath her the earth trembled with the pounding of men and horses, and she closed her eyes in terror.

Spears and swords flashing, the soldiers closed in, seeking the men among the enemy. Though if a woman or child got in the way, that was too bad because they were all troublemakers who had no business being there in the first place. This time, however, they had orders that were explicit and firm: Bring in Zebediah, alive or in pieces.

Most of the people went fleeing in either direction along the bank of the river, but only a few of these escaped the pursuing Romans. Others, driven by mindless desperation, ran right into the oncoming troops and were slaughtered. Still others plunged into the dark waters of the river, frantically straining to reach the far side.

Amid this terror and confusion, Zebediah stood with one arm upraised, as if trying to direct attention to himself. Which was, indeed, his intent. "Here!" he shouted, his voice drowned out by the uproar of the one-sided battle. "Here! I am Zebediah! I am the one you seek!"

Incredibly enough, he stood there unnoticed. As if he was somehow invisible to enemy eyes. Jarel kept tugging frantically at his arm, trying to lead him away as he had before, but Zebediah would not be moved.

"Have you seen Rachel?" Zebediah shouted.

Jarel shook his head helplessly.

"Go then!" the prophet instructed, pointing toward the river. "Save yourself!"

"Not without you," Jarel answered.

Seeing the resolution on Jarel's face, Zebediah issued a new directive. "Then find Rachel and lead her to safety. I will meet you on the other side of the river. Go now…Go!"

Dismissing Jarel with this charge, Zebediah made his way down toward the river, all the while calling to the Romans. There, in the midst of the stream that had for so long been to him as a loadstone, he was finally discovered.

Marcellus Servianus Portius, following on horseback some distance behind the main body of the troops, was the one who spied him.

"Zebediah!" he breathed with certainty, though he had never laid eyes on the man before. Kicking at his horse, he went galloping down the slope, through the wide-eyed fleeing people, past the shouts and curses of pursuing soldiers, his hands closed in a death grip about the reins, which the horse now seemed to control.

Zebediah saw him coming. Hurrying to get the last of his people behind him, he went wading forth to meet the horseman, holding out his arms in a gesture of peace.

Just before he swung the sword, Marcellus Servianus thought he saw the old man smile. Then his mount carried him rushing past the target, and his sword swept back before him strangely tinged with rust. Swiveling about, he saw the stump of Zebediah's arm and knew it was not rust that stained the blade but the same red so dark it was almost black that gushed from the severed hand out onto the water.

Choking, he jerked at the reins and swung his horse in a tight, wheeling pattern. As he whirled around and around in the churning spray, he saw the calm, broken smile, the hand disappearing beneath the surface, and the body of the man called Zebediah pitching forward into the dark, bloody waters of final redemption.

XXI

Piercing rays of sunlight slanted across Rachel's eyes, causing her to shut them even more tightly. When she forced them open again, she saw strange men towering above her. One of them crouched down beside her, examining her closely, then looked up at his comrades with a sly grin.

Sounds of trampling feet and pounding hooves and cries of terror and pain filtered through the circle of legs, but a more private horror was descending upon her. Leering faces dripping awful words and phrases blotted out the sky; the smell of sweat and leather and something furiously male closed in about her, covering her like a dirty blanket. Arching her back, she cried out to the Lord to save her.

A savior, of sorts, appeared.

"Halt!" he ordered.

The rapacious group was not of a collective mind to be interrupted. One of them reached for his sword, ready to make a swift end of the intruder.

"Put your sword away!" Justinian Flavius ordered, determined this time to remain in control.

At the sight of their commanding officer sitting above them astride his horse, the errant troops jumped up and straggled to attention.

Flavius glanced briefly at Rachel, who was desperately trying to rearrange her torn clothing, then fixed the offenders with an icy stare. "You men deserted the battle," he declared.

"We…the battle was obviously won, sir," one of the men stammered. "We were merely claiming the spoils of victory…"

"You explain your actions too loosely!" Justinian shot back. "And, at any rate, spoils are claimed only upon permission of the commander. And I gave no such consent!"

The soldiers shifted about uneasily, carefully avoiding all eye contact with either the officer or the intended object of their now rapidly receding lust.

It was into this scene that Marcellus Servianus came riding, his face flushed with excitement. Taking no notice of what was going on, he started to blurt out his story only to be halted by an uplifted aristocratic hand, which pointed first at the girl and then at the group of foot soldiers. With a heroic display of self-control, he stifled the news he was bursting to tell.

"A most unseemly display," Flavius intoned, spurring his horse slowly back and forth, putting on even more of a show now that his aide was in attendance. "A disgrace to the standard you bear. And yet…" he paused, not wanting to undermine morale by being overly severe on his men, and looked over at the girl, "…not entirely beyond understanding. Bring her to her feet," he ordered, and when this was done, he studied her openly and deliberately.

"You may stop sniveling," he told her when his inspection was completed. "No one will harm you. These men were merely…overcome by the moment."

Turning to Marcellus, who was so frantically eager to tell of the marvelous thing he had done that he could barely keep his seat on the horse, Flavius instructed his aide to take charge of the girl and bring her back to the garrison, and then shifted his attention back to the other men.

"Return to the task at hand," he ordered. "And consider yourself fortunate that it was I who was in command," he added, feeling certain his dismissal of the affair would win him favor with his troops. Having so spoken, he turned his horse back toward the incline where he might better observe the slaughter.

Marcellus Servianus watched incredulously as Flavius rode away. He started to spur after him, turned back toward he girl, started to spur off again, then halted a second time. His horse, wanting to go one way or the other, began to wheel about in a tight little circle, moving faster and faster until Marcellus Servianus feared he might slip off the saddle. Suddenly realizing he still had one hand thrust in the air, he let it fall with an exasperated cry, then screamed for his horse to stop.

XXII

From somewhere far off there came the low neighing of a horse, and Cestus rose up on one elbow, instantly alert.

The first pale light of morning filtered through the tent. He looked past it intently, but the morning was quiet. Perhaps he had imagined the sound, he thought. Or dreamed it. There had been so many sounds of danger that they followed him everywhere, even in his sleep. Still, the day you let down your guard was the day you died, so he slipped from the warmth of the bedding.

"Where are you going?" the woman beside him murmured, seeking him with her hand. She was the product of blood from more than one race, the mingling of which had produced high cheekbones, exotic green eyes, and tawny skin pulled tight over a body that robbed men of their breath.

Cestus had liberated her from the leader of a clan who had made the mistake of trying to raid his people. Just before the last full moon, a band of horsemen had swept down upon the camp, intending to gather horses and perhaps a woman or two and make a quick escape. Instead they found themselves quickly routed and fleeing for their lives.

The leader of the raiders led a panicked flight back to his encampment, where he ended up losing his horse, his own woman, and several of his men. He escaped with his life only because he was knocked unconscious during the fray and Cestus was not in a mood to kill him in that state and so had simply ridden away, taking the exotic-looking woman with him.

"Be quiet, Sharra..." Cestus said, putting a finger to his lips.

The woman sat up in alarm but made no further sound. Unlike her former mate, this one was neither ugly nor cruel, and as she watched him gather his sword and bow, she felt concern for his safety.

Cestus pulled back the flap of his tent and stepped outside. In the gray half-light, the campsite seemed peaceful and secure. Tents were closed and undisturbed, the dark shadows of the horse pen were still. Near a burned-out campfire a dog lay sleeping. Could he have heard, he wondered, what the animals had not?

Everything appeared in order, yet some instinct told him otherwise. Besides, he was wide awake now, so he went to his horse and slowly began to stroke its mane, still listening with one ear as he considered some things that had been weighing on his mind, things which the day gave him little time to reflect on.

Soon they must break camp. Where they were now, not far from the great shimmering water, was good in many ways, but there were too many people nearby, too many towns filled with eyes and tongues. So they must move on, leave the lowlands for the mountain heights. Let the hot months pass there.

And then?

Here he halted, unaccustomed to looking that far into the future. For himself it mattered little which path he took, but now there were others to consider. Others who had gathered about him, who depended on him and would follow his lead no matter in which direction, and so there were no longer easy decisions.

After he had slain Titus in the arena, he had been granted release, just as Antonius Cappio had promised. Quickly, before the promise might be taken back, he had enlisted the help of Braccus to purchase a horse and weapons with the coins of his fame that he had been allowed to keep. Then he rode, leaving Rome as far and as quickly behind as he could. For the most part he simply wandered, following no set course because he seldom knew where he was, much less where he was going.

Though he did not seek them, he gradually accumulated companions. First there came a lone horseman who rode alongside for a while, the two measuring one another carefully until it was agreed by mutual and silent consent that two were better protection against other men and beasts than one. Then a former slave who had recently liberated himself joined the pair near a small coastal village that had been harassed by pirates. Because the trio had no reason not to, they stayed long enough to organize resistance. And when the plunderers returned, it was for the last time. The day after the battle was over, two more rode with them, strong young men eager for adventure. Others attached themselves along the way, peasants and farmers and runaway slaves, some with women and children, and now and then a warrior, all looking to the same man for something they recognized but did not possess.

Now as that man gazed about the camp, he reflected on how large it was, how many people it contained, how many tents and animals and campfires. Perhaps, he whispered aloud to his horse, it had become too large. Perhaps he should turn over leadership of the clan to one of the others and ride away with nothing, not even the woman.

The sound came again, this time close and distinct. Squinting through the swirling mist of dawn, he saw its source: the gnarled chieftain whose former woman lay at that moment in a tent near the center of the camp. He was on the distant side of a small brook that ran alongside the edge of the campsite, flanked on both sides by members of his clan.

For the briefest of moments, Cestus wondered why the other man would come back here again when he had barely escaped death the first time. No doubt he counted on the cover of darkness and surprise to help in his quest for revenge, he thought, and then he dismissed all thought.

Mounting his horse, he urged it forward, answering the unspoken call.

At the sight of his foe, the chieftain hesitated, knowing he had lost the element of surprise. Then, having come too far to back down, he raised his battle axe and roared out a challenge.

"I come to claim my woman!" he shouted. "And your life!" he added, glancing quickly at the horsemen on either side of him.

Cestus's nostrils flared, his body stiffened, and he laughed.

Facing an armed and savage bunch of horsemen on a morning soon to be filled with death, he laughed.

Some of the men of the clan were hurrying out of their tents, but Cestus did not wait for them. He would rather have taken on the fool—and a double fool he was, first for returning to seek revenge and second for sitting there bellowing out his intent—at closer quarters, but the other man was raising his hand in a signal to attack. Holding his horse steady, Cestus notched an arrow to his bowstring and took aim.

The chieftain stretched his battle axe toward the sky and let out a roar... then arm and voice faltered in unison, the declaration of war cut short by the savage entry of the thin shaft that sped through the soft shadows of the awakening day and across the rippling brook to penetrate his fleshy neck.

Astounded that the arrow had found its mark at such a distance, the men on either side of the chieftain watched in stunned disbelief as their leader groped haltingly at the silent winged killer protruding from his throat before sliding lifelessly to the ground. Relieved of its burden, the horse went trotting away, and the would-be attackers quickly followed. They were all good fighters, they would later assure themselves. As brave as any. But no man could fight a magician.

When the people of Cestus's clan saw what he had done, they came rushing up to him in exultation, jumping and dancing about and calling out his name in a chanting wave of praise that filled his ears and mind. And as the separate voices became one and rose in pitch and volume, he was transported back to the bloody circle of sand and a great wall of faceless people filling seats that rose up to the edge of the sky, shouting out the same word-name of death as he stood rooted, unable to escape that moment from which there was no return.

XXIII

Lucius Portius had been intending to make the journey for nearly a year, but one thing after another kept getting in his way. At first he had deliberately delayed in order to allow Marcellus Servianus time to accustom himself to his new surroundings. After a suitable period, he began preparations for travel. But winter came early and with such force that his plans had to be canceled. When the weather became at last more cooperative, Claudia came down with a lingering illness that made a planned absence by her husband most unseemly.

So it had been more than a year since he had last seen his son, a circumstance he had not foreseen and had Claudia so fretful and incensed that she was making noises about being allowed to accompany him on the eastern journey. Thus he hurriedly completed preparations. And when he departed, it was with the promise to Claudia that their son would be with him on the return passage.

He took the overland route, a trip that required some sixty days and left him with the inescapable conclusion that he was not nearly as young as he used to be.

Upon reaching his destination, he was immediately escorted to headquarters, where he found to his dismay that Marcellus Servianus was absent. It seemed the younger Portius had departed a few days before for the lower regions of Judea, riding once again as second-in-command to Justinian Flavius in pursuit of the elusive Zebediah.

When the two young officers arrived back at the garrison, they found that Lucius Portius had been there several days, awaiting their return. Much to their relief, when the esteemed senator and general was ushered into their presence, he showed not even a hint of annoyance at the delay.

"Ah, Marcellus, it is good to see you," he said, embracing his son. "You are looking well."

"Thank you. It is good to see you, father," Marcellus replied. "I regret that I could not be here when you arrived."

"No apology needed," the elder Portius said. "The garrison commander informed me that you were on a mission of some importance."

Turning to Justinian Flavius, Portius clasped him on the shoulder. "And you, Tribune," he said, the tone of his voice far more cordial than official. "I trust that all is going well…"

"Yes, exceptionally well, General, thank you."

Portius stepped back, still smiling. "Well…?" he said, addressing both of them at once.

Once again Marcellus Servianus was bursting to tell, but he managed to keep quiet, allowing Justinian Flavius to give the report, as was his right of rank.

"We have just returned from an expedition in search of a band of zealots headed by the notorious Zebediah," Flavius began. "I am pleased to report that the zealots were located and completely routed. I am even more pleased to report that the rebel Zebediah has been disposed of for once and for all—and by the hand of none other than Marcellus Servianus."

This latter bit of information was so stunning that Lucius Portius was only peripherally aware of the rest of Flavius's flowery summation. "That is splendid news!" he blurted when Flavius finished his recital. "Absolutely splendid! Since the two of you have acquitted yourselves so well, you deserve a reward. And so your tour of duty here is coming to an end. When I return to Rome, both of you will accompany me. I trust," he added wryly, "that you will not mind having to move out on such short notice."

The Tribune and his aide were so elated by the news that they later attempted to markedly reduce the garrison's supply of wine. Somewhere in the midst of their revelry, Flavius had an inspiration. During his unfortunate stay as a guest at Alba Longa, he had gained an insight into his host's sexual inclinations. Now a bright light in the dense fog of his brain illuminated a way in which he might further ingratiate himself to the elder Portius, and perhaps involve him in a folly of his own.

That week a new serving girl appeared at the officer's dining hall. She had been made especially presentable for the occasion, and at her entrance Roman mouths hung open, eyes widened, and the labor of the cooks was momentarily forgotten.

Tribune Flavius discretely studied Lucius Portius as the girl went about her duties, and then leaned toward him in a conspiratorial manner. "She is an attractive young thing, isn't she?" he commented. "I came upon her during the raid on Zebediah," he went on. "In point of fact, I rescued her and had her brought here. It was my thought that she might serve any manner of purposes, but now…now I would be honored if you would accept her as a present from me. I will gladly make arrangements to have her delivered to your home or your estate at Alba Longa, whichever you prefer."

The elder Portius responded with raised eyebrows.

"Let's just say that the gesture is a small token of my appreciation for all you have done for me in the name of friendship," Flavius said. "And, quite frankly, I hope it may atone in some small manner for any embarrassment that the, uh, situation at your villa may have caused."

"I assure you that little matter has been long forgotten," Portius replied, his eyes lingering on the servant girl.

Since the hour of her capture, Rachel had prayed day and night for deliverance. Her prayers were not only for herself, however; she always included others in her supplications: her mother, her departed father, family and friends and those who were in need, saving Zebediah for last, not knowing if he was alive or not but fearing the worst.

Though her daily devotions did not bring her physical deliverance, they at least gave her some solace of mind and spirit. Then came word that she was to be sent to the land of the Romans.

The trip from Caesarea to Rome could take from as little as twenty to more than sixty days, depending on weather conditions and method of travel—sea, land, or a combination of both. Rachel and three other handpicked slaves were to be transported by ship. The very thought of embarking on a journey upon such an immense mass of water filled Rachel's mind with terrifying images of a dark, wind-driven sea surging beneath a black sky roaring with thunder and lightning, of slipping under the billowing waves and sinking, choking and helpless, to an unmarked, watery grave.

Her prayers became ever more desperate, but as the hour of departure grew near, she had to concede that it was too late.

As if to cement her fate, the morning before departure she was sent to assist in keeping a record of provisions being delivered to the ship. She trudged alongside a large donkey cart containing the supplies, her eyes and heart downcast, oblivious to the clear blue sky, the magnificent walls and towers of the harbor, the sunlight-dappled waters of the Mediterranean.

The cart halted before a towering vessel, and the driver ordered a handful of waiting workers to unload the cart and take the contents to the ship's galley. As each container was removed from the cart Rachel made a mark with a stylus on a wax tablet as she had been instructed. In less than an hour the task was completed and the workers departed.

The driver pulled a heavy sheet of canvas over the empty cart and ran a hand over his sweaty beard. "Well, now," he said to Rachel, letting his eyes run over her appraisingly, "I have to return to Nazareth with this cart. But first, I'm going to refresh myself with some wine. It's a pity you can't join me..."

When Rachel made no reply, he turned, crossed a walkway, and headed for what Rachel supposed was a tavern of sorts. She started to trek back to the barracks, paused to watch the driver enter a doorway, moved on a few steps more, then paused again and looked back at the cart. Without giving it any further thought, she scampered to the wagon, looked around, lifted the canvas cover, and quickly slipped beneath it.

It seemed an eternity before she heard the driver return. She felt him take his seat on the wagon, and heard him give a sharp order to the donkey. The wagon began to move, slowly and joltingly, and she braced herself, fearing that any moment the cart would be halted, the cover pulled back, and she would be discovered.

Panic overwhelmed her; the canvas seemed to sink in upon her, smothering, cutting off her breath. Suddenly, the cart came to a halt.

She stiffened, closed her eyes, unable to face the inevitable. Male voices, loud and jocular, came closer. "So, what are you smuggling out of here today?" one of them boomed, and Rachel knew it must be a guard at the city gate.

"Hah! Two slave wenches and a barrel of wine," the driver replied. "Look for yourself, if you like. But hurry; I have to be in Nazareth by nightfall."

"Nazareth! You have my sympathy. Pass on, then. But on your return, bring the wenches back to us. Since they're in your hands I'm sure they'll be unused!"

It was not until well after the noon hour before it was noted that Rachel had not returned from the harbor. A search of the barracks and grounds was conducted, and she was nowhere to be found. Ordinarily a runaway slave girl might not have been considered worth the trouble of pursuit, but in this case half a dozen foot soldiers and two horsemen were dispatched. Their orders were brief and to the point: Find the girl and bring her back unharmed.

Though she had made it beyond the walls of Caesarea, Rachel lay stiff and unmoving, scarcely daring to breathe. Nazareth, the driver had said. He was going to Nazareth, not far from her home town of Besara. Minutes became an hour. Her body ached from tension and the wooden bed of the of cart; the midday heat was smothering beneath the blanket of canvas; dust raised by the wheels of the cart somehow seeped inside, causing her to pinch her nose violently to keep from sneezing. After what she thought must have been at least an hour, she dared to move enough to peek out under the front of the canvas. The driver was hunched over, his back to her, facing the path the donkey was taking.

She painstakingly inched to the rear of the cart, took a deep breath, wiggled out, and landed on her hands and knees. Swiveling her head around, she saw that the cart was continuing on its way. She crabbed backward a few yards, keeping low. Then she got to her feet and broke into a run, racing toward a low rise of hills opposite the distant shoreline, until she outdistanced her breath. After a brief and frantic pause, she forced herself on, tripping over things unseen, driven by visions of wild animals crouched in waiting, of bandits and other evil men lurking behind every hill, of horses bearing armed men coming in pursuit.

Only when she could absolutely not go on did Rachel stop to rest. Her lungs were burning, her body aching, but more than anything, she was tormented by thirst. She had no idea how far she was from the safety of Gedar; she only knew she had to get moving again—and that she had to find water. Within the desert of her mouth there was not a trace of moisture; her swollen throat ached with the passage of each dusty breath. And when she tried to wet her parched lips with her tongue, it was like rubbing dry leaves together.

She pushed herself upright and stumbled on.

Just when it seemed she could endure no more, she heard a low gurgling sound. She struggled to the top of a ridge, hoping to get a clearer view of her surroundings. There, below, she saw the wondrous source of the sound: a sun-dappled trickling stream that formed a little pool in a basin of rock.

With a hoarse cry of thanksgiving she hurried to the pool and plunged her face into its shallow depths, drinking deeply of the cool, sweet water, letting it flow over her chin and neck and down onto her shoulders and breasts. Thank you, Lord, she whispered, her eyes closed in rapture. Thank you.

Then she heard another sound.

Rising up, she saw the heart-stopping form of a Roman soldier.

She blinked rapidly, certain it had to be a mirage, but it did not go away. Uttering a moan of despair, she jumped up and started to run away, but other soldiers appeared, two of them on horseback. Sweating and shouting and grinning in triumph, they closed in about her.

From the cover of a stand of trees, three other men on horseback watched the drama unfold.

"Romans!" one of them said, spitting out the word.

The one who was their leader nodded, then notched an arrow to his bow. "We are all free men here," he said, turning to the men who rode beside him. "Do as you choose."

By way of answer, the two unsheathed their swords.

At the sight of the unknown approaching horsemen, the officer in charge of the Roman patrol alerted his men and rode his own horse forward.

"Go on your way!" he ordered. "This woman escaped from Roman custody at the fortress in Caesarea. We have been sent to return her."

None of the three horsemen made any reply. They were fierce-looking men, the officer thought. Hard-eyed and well-armed. And, most unusual for men of this region, they rode horses.

"Are you deaf and mute? Or do you not understand?" he shouted, determined to show them, no matter who they were, that the Legion was not to be taken lightly. "Leave us now or suffer the consequences!"

At this, one of the three opened his mouth. "I understand your words," he said. "Now understand mine. My name is Cestus. And I take no orders from Romans!"

The name apparently did not register with the Roman, but the insult did. "Then die!" he shot back. And at his signal, the four foot soldiers advanced, spears at ready above their shields, and the other cavalryman swept in alongside him, their swords unsheathed and flashing.

Cestus unleashed a single arrow. The closest cavalryman took the sharp point in his throat and carried it past his intended prey in the sightless grip of death. Leaving the other cavalryman to his comrades, Cestus put away the bow and went raging with the sword, trailing an unearthly howl of fury and joy.

When a Roman search party came upon the unfortunate detachment just before sunset, they found one man still alive. After they had revived him and tended to his wounds, he related what had happened.

"The one who led them was a demon!" he mumbled in dazed conclusion. "A demon from hell if ever there was one! He called himself Cestus," he added. And even at such a great distance from the arenas of Rome there were those among the troops who knew the name well.

XXIV

The Romans were good fighters. One of his men had tasted a Roman spear, and the other had nearly lost his horse. Had it not been for the power of his own arm, Cestus thought, three against eight might have been fatal odds.

The Romans were also many in number, and so the clan must move quickly and retrace their steps to the north and seek again the mountain heights. Once they were well clear of this place they should be safe enough.

There was no time to waste, so they hurriedly broke camp. When they came to a new stopping place they would consider what to do with the girl they had rescued. Meanwhile, she was taken under the fleshy, protective wing of a large and homely woman known only as Lavinia. Still new to the clan herself, Lavinia eagerly adopted the task of looking after this latest addition.

Still new to the clan herself, Lavinia eagerly adopted the task of looking after this latest addition. "Stay by my side," she said as the band made its rapid decampment. "Tonight, when we stop, we'll have time to talk." Then, seeing the naked fear and despair in the girl's eyes, Lavinia paused and gave her a smile. "You will be all right," she assured. "You are safer here than you think."

The people traveled in a column, with warriors at either end and the women, children and supplies in-between The clan halted well before nightfall and made a secure camp, with sentries posted on all sides. Small cooking fires were lit and food prepared and eaten, then the people lay down to rest. By then Lavinia had recovered enough wind to give Rachel a briefing on the clan. Food and duties were shared so that no one went without either. When necessary, contention among members of the clan were settled by decision of a three man council. Most important, each person was regarded as free, able to stay or leave as they chose, with the understanding that remaining meant observing the rules. Overall, the clan was something like a big family, Lavinia explained. Once you were taken into it, you had a place. You belonged and were protected.

All of this, Lavinia emphasized, came about through the one called Cestus. He had been the most famous gladiator in all of Rome, she said, her voice taking on a tone that was something beyond simple admiration.

"Gladiator?" Rachel said, not understanding the word.

"Gladiators are…they're warriors who fight each other in the arena."

"What is this arena?"

"Well, I myself have never seen one. But from what I hear, they are very big buildings built in a circle. The center is open, and that's where the fighting contests take place. Around this open center are rows of seats where people sit to watch the contests. I have heard that in the city of Rome there is an arena so big there are contests with chariots pulled by horses." She shook her head. "Can you imagine such a place?"

"Why do they do such a thing?" Rachel asked.

"Why do they watch?"

"No, why do they fight?"

"Because they are slaves, and that was what they must do."

"This Cestus must have fought well. I saw what he did to the Roman soldiers," Rachel said.

"From what I hear, he was the best of them all. Word is he fought so well that he won his freedom by killing the personal bodyguard of the emperor of Rome in the arena. But that doesn't make any sense to me. I would think that killing the emperor's own bodyguard would have brought Cestus death as well.

"So, anyway, after winning his freedom, he got a horse and rode wherever the wind took him. Then one day the man who was wounded today in your rescue came to join him. In time, more and more came. Mostly slaves—some of us were escaping, and some of us were rescued. Now Cestus is the leader of this clan. He is a great warrior," Lavinia gushed. "A great leader. And," she sighed, "as handsome as a god…"

This last thought seemed to drain her of the last of her energy, and Lavinia rolled over in her blanket and closed her eyes. "Try to sleep," she mumbled, her last advice of the day.

Four times the sun rose on makeshift camps. By the fifth day, they were in the highlands, far from the sight of the Romans. And when they came upon a shallow brook, they set up camp and rested. Only then did Cestus invite the new girl to his tent to talk.

Lavinia took over preparations for the occasion. First she took Rachel some distance downstream, where she dumped jars of water over her shivering body, keeping a sharp watch for prying eyes. Then she combed and braided Rachel's hair, and finally she introduced Rachel to the art of makeup as practiced by the women of the clan. When all was in order, she produced a clean tunic. And by skillful tucking and gathering and belting, Lavinia made the oversized garment look almost as if it had been especially designed for the much smaller figure she was fitting it to.

Through it all Rachel squirmed in protest, but when it was done and a small mirror held before her eyes, she allowed a smile. Then she impulsively reached out and gave her new friend a hug, needing to hold someone close if only for a moment.

"Remember, no harm will come to you here," Lavinia whispered.

Lavinia's assurances notwithstanding, Rachel made her way on trembling legs. When she reached the designated tent, she paused. Taking in a deep breath, she took the final step.

Cestus was not alone. He and the two men with him rose to their feet as she entered. "I am called Cestus," he said. "These are the other two members of the council. Malameus and Rolf," nodding in turn toward the sinewy, dark haired man on his right and the towering, thick-bodied warrior on his left. He motioned to a cushion covered couch. "Please…sit."

The tent was surprisingly large and comfortable, with braziers for light and warmth, brightly colored rugs to cover the earthen floor, and cushions to serve as couches, but Rachel took little notice of her surroundings. Moving to the indicated place, she sat stiffly, nervously trying not to think.

"Do you speak in Latin?" Cestus said, asking the question in that tongue, not knowing if the girl was of the Roman world, only that he had taken her from there.

"I…my people speak in the Hebrew tongue," she replied haltingly. "But I can manage a little in Greek."

"Greek I can manage a little also," he said, switching to that language. "And there are those among us who know the words of your people. You are called Rachel…"

"Yes," Rachel answered, wondering how Cestus could move so easily from one tongue to another.

"That is not a Roman name…"

"No. I am from the village of Besara, in Galilee."

Cestus nodded, but gave no indication that he had ever heard of such a place. "How did it come to pass that the Roman soldiers were pursuing you?"

Rachel cleared her throat, looked down at the floor, and began.

As he listened to Rachel describe the events at the river and beyond, Cestus found himself thinking that the most ornamented female in all of Rome, painted and powdered and perfumed, could not begin to compare to the woman now before him. Nor could any he had seen in the many towns and villages of his passing. Not even the one who now shared his tent and was considered alluring above all others. When he realized such thoughts were drowning out her words, he fixed his gaze on a spot just beyond her head and kept it there.

At the conclusion of her narrative, Rachel paused, and then slowly raised her eyes to the face of her inquisitor.

"Now I would like to ask you a question," she said.

Cestus nodded. "Ask."

"Why did you risk your life to save mine?"

"You were a lone woman, pursued by soldiers. What we did was no more than what had to be done. Besides, I, too, was once a captive of the Romans."

At the end of Rachel's meeting with Cestus, Lavinia was waiting anxiously in their tent. "So, tell me what happened," she blurted.

"They questioned me."

"They?"

"Cestus and two other men."

"Oh. The council. That was the council. Well, what then?"

"Then Cestus told me I was welcome to remain with the clan if I wished."

"And...you mean that was all?"

"That was all." Rachel went to her pallet and lay down and closed her eyes, visibly sagging with relief. "Why?" she asked after a moment. "You sound surprised."

"Surprised!" Lavinia threw her hands up in mock exasperation. "Surprised, she says! On one hand we have Cestus, the strongest and most handsome of warriors. And on the other we have you..." She molded the air in the time-honored gesture of a shapely woman. "And what happens when he calls you to his tent? Nothing but questions!" She shook her head slowly from side to side, enjoying her own performance.

"They say," she went on, "that he is even better on the couch than on the battlefield. Well, all I know is that if he ever calls me to his tent, I'll not leave until he proves his reputation!"

Rachel blushed furiously at this, a reaction that caused Lavinia to burst out laughing.

"Look at you," she teased. "Your cheeks are flaming like those of a virgin!" She stopped short, halted by her own words.

Rachel's averted eyes and silence provided the answer.

Buttoning her mouth, Lavinia went over and stretched out on her own pallet, where she lapsed into a deep and prolonged—and most uncustomary—silence, contemplating the ever-changing mysteries of a world she thought she had almost deciphered.

Rachel finally broke the quiet. "It is so strange," she said, almost as if speaking to herself. "When Cestus fought the Roman soldiers it seemed the fury of a demon was unleashed. Yet, when the battle was over, and he put me on his horse, the fury was gone and his hands were gentle. And now, in his tent, his manner was kind and his voice was soft." She propped up on an elbow and looked over at Lavinia as if searching for an answer. "It is like there are two different men in one body."

After the council broke up, Cestus sat alone in his tent for a while, unable to dismiss thoughts of the girl named Rachel. Ever since he had swept her atop his horse after the fight with the Romans, he had been unable to get her out of his mind, even though he had tried to deny all thoughts of her through the worried miles of flight. Why, he wondered now, did he not take the opportunity to be alone with her instead of calling in the others of the council?

Was it because of the green-eyed woman named Sharra who now shared his tent? Every time the new girl came into view, her face hardened. But no, that was not the reason. Though Sharra was pleasing in many ways, he did not hold himself in check only because of her. Rather, it had to do with the new girl herself. There was something different about her, something indefinable that made her somehow unlike any woman he had ever seen.

Thus he decided to let matters unravel themselves, as most things did, given enough time. Having so resolved, he glanced up to see Sharra, she of the hard-green eyes, at the entrance to his tent.

Silently she inquired if she might enter.

Silently he consented.

XXV

He must be getting old, Lucius Portius thought gloomily. The trip to the eastern frontier had left him listless and fatigued for days on end. A lack of energy was not the main symptom on which he based his diagnosis of aging, however. Nor were the various aches and pains he had accumulated during the journey. Far worse was a dwindling enthusiasm for the three things that had long been the foremost interests of his life.

To begin with, several times in recent days, the thought had actually occurred to him that in all truth he had more than enough money to last several lifetimes. And with this thought came the nagging and unanswerable question of why, then, did he continue to put himself through the daily and increasingly more difficult struggle to acquire more—more money, more property, more artifacts, more horses, more slaves—instead of simply relaxing and enjoying all that he had?

Moreover, several times since his return to Rome, he had found himself sitting in the senate chambers thinking that the matters being debated before that august body were not only trifling but also excruciatingly boring. The more such thoughts repeated themselves, the more they led to the inescapable conclusion that the arena of politics in which he had so long immersed himself had lost its luster, had become for him a vessel filled with wine gone rancid.

Perhaps worst of all, not once since he had returned from his journey to the east had he engaged in sexual activity. Not, that is, to completion of the act. Had it been merely a question of lack of congress with Claudia, it would have of less concern. The barriers between them had grown so thick and many that he avoided her bedchamber except on rare occasions, and then he found little pleasure except in forcing her to do his will. But now the sporadic failure that, he assured himself, might be expected of a man his age had become not the exception but the status quo.

He had visited with the woman who, before his departure, had been his latest mistress; and rather than an occasion of pleasure, it had turned out to be an evening of frustration and embarrassment. A few days later, he had summoned a nubile young household slave, but he remained flaccid and unable to come to release.

If such thoughts and failings persisted, he told himself, he might as well lie down and close his eyes. When neither money nor politics nor sex interested him, there would be no need to call for a physician; the end would be undeniably near.

Meanwhile, however, tired and dispirited though he might be, Portius was nonetheless a man of some discipline. There were serious matters to attend to, matters demanding his personal action, so he turned his face toward the tasks at hand.

Of immediate concern was the future of his only son, which was in turn the future of the Portius name, the Portius family fortunes. By all accounts, Marcellus Servianus had acquitted himself well in Palestine under the tutelage of Justinian Flavius. He had acquired experience in foreign service and, wonder of wonders, on the field of battle. Indeed, he had performed so well that upon his return to Rome, he had been granted the rank of tribune. Now, however, it was time to separate the two young men, for the one had served his purpose.

Young Flavius had made it abundantly clear that he coveted a return to the Praetorian Guard, a position that could be easily arranged. Such station would likely be as far as Flavius would rise in the military, but his career was no longer of consequence.

Of course, Marcellus Servianus would also much prefer a post with the Guard, with its ease and privilege of duty. He would also, his father thought darkly, prefer to idle about the house, eating and drinking unwisely and sleeping until noon. Since returning home, Marcellus had appeared but once at the equestrian area, and then only briefly in order to display the skill he had so recently acquired. Even more disturbing was the fact that he had attended but a single session of the senate, and that in the company of Flavius to present the Legion report.

When he mentioned such things to his wife, she replied (siding as always with her son) that he should not be so hard on the boy (the fact that she referred to him as boy rankled the senior Portius even more, but he clamped down on his tongue). Marcellus would all too soon be weighed down with the tedium of duty, she said. For the present he should be allowed to enjoy his days of youth. Such days were all too brief, she declared, her voice rising shrilly, and when they were gone, they were gone forever.

Thus isolated within his cage of disappointment, Lucius Portius continued to plot the fortunes of his family and his son. If only, he fretted again and again, "the boy" was not so stubbornly resistant to discipline. Though, to give him his due, he had made considerable progress in the past year. Plus, of course, he was as inherently capable as any other young man his age. For he was, after all, a Portius. Not that sheer capability was necessarily of primary importance. For if a man succeeded on ability alone, there would be few leaders in Rome or anywhere else. No, in due time, Marcellus Servianus would scale such heights as had been planned for him. He had only to learn to drink from the cup of discipline—and from the goblet of ambition as well. All the rest could be arranged.

But this much he had to understand clearly: His father was still the one who would do the arranging.

XXVI

Sharra's mirror, her most prized possession, told her that her looks had not changed. Her face, her eyes, her hair, and her body were the same as before.

The eyes of the men of the clan told her the same.

But something had changed within Cestus.

Of course, the answer was plain to see. Still, she denied it. Refused to accept that it could possibly be so.

Never since she had shed the body of a young girl for that of a young woman had she lost a male to another female.

And never in her life had she wanted a man like she coveted Cestus.

So overwhelming was the desire, the deep aching need, that she—who had considered men the enemy, creatures conferred with brute power that they swiftly bartered away to fulfill their unthinking desire for the other, greater, power she possessed—came to understand those women who said they could not live without their man.

She knew she could easily find a place with another male of the clan, but that would be no better than the fate she had endured more than once before. No, it would be worse than before, now that she had known Cestus.

As for the females of the clan, she had not bothered herself to befriend a single one of them. So she had no place, neither within the clan nor outside of it.

She had been set aside. Rejected. Replaced by another.

Jealousy and humiliation cohabited, coupled to produce a red-eyed fury from which there was no release. The thought of vengeance woke her in the morning, walked beside her throughout the day, and lay down with her again at night, a constant and loveless companion.

She imagined countless scenes of revenge...saw in the hard and narrow eye of her mind herself lying in wait, her fingers wrapped tightly about the handle of a knife...saw Rachel come walking along the path, unknowing...saw and felt the thrust of the knife...saw and felt and heard the whore of the Romans dying the death she deserved.

More than once she actually picked up a knife as if to fulfill the deed, but she knew that the act of killing Rachel would not bring Cestus back to her.

Nor would it extract the full measure of vengeance she sought.

No. For that, both of them must die. Not just the one. Or the other. But both.

And so she abided, swallowing her hurt and humiliation until the time she would be able to bring about the act of palliation.

She knew it would not be easy to accomplish, for Cestus was very powerful. Beside him, even the chieftain who had formerly claimed her had been as a child in battle.

No, it would not be easy. But it would be done.

Though Rachel was unaware of Sharra's raging fury, she was nonetheless troubled in mind and in spirit. She was, she agonized, living in sin. There had been no ceremony of marriage according to the custom of her people, no observance of time-honored rituals. The clan had their customs, and so she had simply come into Cestus's tent.

At his invitation.

Of her own accord.

How could it, then, be sin?

The answer lay in ancient teachings.

But the men who taught such things had been old, with long, white beards and dark, black robes. And now they were dead, while she and Cestus were alive, drinking from the same cup of life overflowing.

And yet she feared the bliss they shared would not last for long.

He was, after all, not of her people. He was not of any people. He had no town or village or country, no place to call his own. He was a wanderer, a nomad. A strange and quiet man whose only god was his sword.

Yet, despite his reputation, she knew no fear when she was with him. Quite the opposite—she had come to feel safe and protected when in his presence. And not only because he had been the one who had rescued her from the Romans, and the one who insured her safety afterward. No, there was something more. Something deeper.

Beneath the fierce exterior the world beheld, she had glimpsed the true man. The inner man. The reluctant warrior, awesome and fierce in battle, but not by his own choosing. The man with a deep but unspoken gentleness and compassion for others that caused him each day to lay down his own self for the good of the clan. It was as if two separate beings inhabited the single body: one that lived there most of the time, and another that possessed it in times of danger.

It was a mystery she did not even begin to understand, but one she could not resist.

And so it was clearly not possible, not even to be thought of, yet it was happening nonetheless.

"What are you thinking?" he asked.

They were lying beneath the willows on the bank of the stream close by their encampment, watching the rise of the moon and the lighting of the stars.

"Nothing really…" she replied.

"Tell me…"

"I was thinking of how you rescued me from the Romans…and how I feared you then."

He rose up on one elbow. "And now?" he said, studying her face in the moonlight.

"Now I know that you are not at all like the man others think you to be. Yet sometimes I think that there are two of you in one. Two separate men inhabiting one body. And I wonder how that can be."

He took her hand in his, and for some time she thought he had retreated before the question into some hidden place where no one else was allowed.

"Many times at night I have sat alone and looked up at the sky," he said at last. "It is so big, the heavens at night. So big and dark and cold, and I feel small and lost and alone beneath it all."

He paused, and Rachel waited without speaking, wondering what such words had to do with her question, and wondering as well that this great warrior, so fierce and strong and seemingly invincible, should confess to such feelings.

"When I first faced a man on the sands of death, a great fear came upon me," he went on. "So great that I thought it would be the cause of my death, but instead it was this fear that saved me."

Again he paused, struggling to find a way to bring his thoughts into her mind, to somehow explain this thing that he had never spoken of before.

"We are all animals in part," he said, "and when the fear comes hard upon me, I call forth my animal being. I loosen the beast that dwells within. I ride the beast through the danger, and when it is past, I rein the beast back in."

"Then what I saw when you fought the Romans was the…the release of a demon?"

He shrugged uncertainly. "I only know it as the beast that dwells within."

"And that…it…enables you to survive?"

"Yes."

"Yet," she said, unsettled by images of demons, of dark and unseen things beyond the world in which she walked, "I sense that you wish to be free of it."

Cestus shrugged. "This thing that comes upon me has enabled me to survive," he replied. "It may be that if it dies, I might die. Even so…yes, I wish there was some other way."

"There is." Rachel said. "There is something that dwells within all of us that is more powerful than this beast you speak of."

"What might that be?"

"The Spirit of God."

"Which god?"

"There is but one God, my beloved."

"One god? Not so. The people of my childhood worshiped a number of gods: The god of the sun…the god of war…the god of fire…the god of the waters. So it is as well with the people of the clan. They each bring with them the gods of their people. Even the Romans have many gods."

"Yes, but none of them are real gods. They are all myths, gods created by people. There is but one true living God, one Creator who made the heavens and the earth and all the things of life. People did not create this god, but rather it was God who created people."

"How is it you speak so surely of such things?" Cestus asked, for the manner in which she spoke said there was no doubt in her mind.

"Because of Zebediah, the holy man I told you about. Those of us who followed him believed that at times he spoke with God. Or rather that God spoke to him."

"Your god spoke to this Zebediah? Appeared and spoke as a man speaks?"

"He spoke to Zebediah, but not as a man speaks. Zebediah told us that God dwells within all men, all people. And that he speaks to us from within. We only have to listen, Zebediah said. Shut out the noise of the world and listen to the voice within."

Cestus released her hand and lay back down, somewhat disappointed that the god of Rachel had not come to life and taken on the form and speech of a man. Now that would have been a god worth hearing about! As far as the matter of a voice speaking to him from within, he himself had often heard words in his head. Sometimes had even answered them. But that was just himself talking to himself, not a god giving him a message. Yet, who could say where these voices truly came from? For indeed there dwelled within his own being a presence other than himself.

He lay there for some time, turning it all over in his mind. At last he sat back up and studied Rachel's face closely.

"What kinds of things did the voice of your god say to this holy man?" he asked.

"There is one who lives in my village who knew this holy man well," she said. "He can tell you what this holy man told him."

XXVII

To his mind it was outrageous. Simply and absolutely and totally outrageous. He had barely re-accustomed himself to life in Rome, to life as it should be lived, before he was told he was being shipped back off again. And to that very same place he had so fervently wished never to hear of again, much less set foot in.

Why? he had angrily demanded, both of the gods that could not be seen and the very visible god that was esteemed general and senator and his father. Why, after he had so well proven himself, must he be sent again to that most distant, most accursed of places?

Because, came the one and only reply he received, it was all part of a master plan for his future. It had all been worked out for the best, the visible god assured.

What was left unsaid was that something was brewing in Palestine. Exactly what, Lucius Portius could not say. By the time various reports reached him, circumstances as often as not had changed. The signs, however, were becoming clearer. Even more significant, his every instinct told him something of great importance was about to happen there. Something that would affect not only the local region but perhaps even the whole of the Empire. If his instinct proved correct, as it usually did, he wanted to be in a position to capitalize on whatever that something was. And Marcellus Servianus would be a perfect conduit for such information.

To help sweeten the move, Marcellus was promised the position of military governor. If all went well, he would in short order return once and for all to the Rome of his choosing, to an assured place in the senate and eventual ownership of all the vast Portius holdings. A little more time, a little more duty, and the rich life was his, a plum that had only to be allowed to fully ripen before it might be plucked.

So he had gone (for what else was he to do?) and for a while had even tried to immerse himself in his duties, to become whatever it was his father wanted him to be. But it was not long before the routine became dull and dreary.

Unbearably dull and dreary.

Sharra had abided throughout the long white season that was winter, remaining with the clan as it left the heights and started the journey toward the lowlands. When they began to come upon settlements and towns, she knew the Romans must be near. And it was the Romans she must seek, for only they had the power to punish Cestus. When she judged she was close enough, she slipped away under cover of darkness, taking with her a supply of food and water and a sharp knife for protection. When morning dawned she was within sight of the walls of a great city.

Sanctuary had been granted her, and with it food and drink to refresh herself. Moreover, in answer to her soft, feminine lament that she was ashamed of her ragged appearance, she was provided with a bath and clean clothing—these latter courtesies extended by an eager young guard hopeful of glimpsing her entering or exiting garments or water or both.

By the time she stepped out of the bath, she had recovered some of the confidence that the splendor and vastness of her new surroundings had eroded. Whoever it was she was to be brought before, in essence he would be like all the other men she had ever known, she assured herself. Powerful or weak, young or old, they were in the end all the same, and this one should be no different.

It was late afternoon on a day that until then had been virtually indistinguishable in its monotony from so many days that had gone before. Except that this one had seemed to Marcellus Servianus to be even longer and duller, if such a thing was possible.

Since shortly after the noon meal he had been sequestered in the judgment hall, listening to matters of legal dispute from the confines of a chair so large and ornate it resembled a throne. Now, as the tedious day drew to a close, he was looking forward to a long bath and a goblet or two of wine. Thus when he was informed that a woman had arrived at the gates seeking sanctuary, and an audience with the official in charge, his initial reaction was to put the matter off. But then, he sighed to himself, if he attended to it today, it would be one less burden he would have to suffer with tomorrow, and so he ordered the woman brought before him.

The moment the guard departed the judgment hall to bring the woman forth, Marcellus Servianus regretted his decision. He should have made her wait until the morrow, he fumed. Or simply refused to see her at all. But before he could issue a change in orders, the doors were thrown open and the woman was brought before him.

In place of the old and ragged creature he had conjured up in his mind, there appeared a young female with a most exotic face and a voluptuous body that exuded raw sexuality. By the time she reached the dais and was granted permission to speak, his head was so filled with scenes of erotica that he scarcely heard a word of her tale of being carried off by a band of barbarians and held captive by their leader, of finally escaping and wandering lost and afraid until fate directed her to the gates of the city.

Even when the woman emphatically declared that the man who had so cruelly mistreated her was a most dangerous enemy of Rome, Marcellus Servianus was inattentive to her words. Only when she pronounced the name of her abductor did the prefect come to attention.

"What was that?" he said, his tone sharp and abrupt.

"I said, my lord, that he is a most dangerous man…"

"No! Not that! His name!"

"He is called Cestus, my lord."

"Are you certain that is his name?"

"Yes. Of that I am certain."

"Did he…do you by chance know if he was ever a gladiator? A fighter in the arena?"

"Why…yes. His people told of him fighting in such a place."

"Describe this man to me," the prefect commanded, now sitting bolt upright on his throne.

The woman did so, carefully omitting any indication that she thought him very handsome. "He is an enemy of Rome," she repeated at the conclusion of her description. "Even while I was held captive by his band, he attacked some Roman soldiers and took away a woman who was their prisoner."

"Yes!" Marcellus Servianus said, lifting up a hand to cut short her recital. "No doubt he is a terrible enemy of Rome!" For some time he looked down at the floor in brooding, chin-stroking silence. Then he raised his eyes and fixed his gaze again upon the woman.

"What did you say your name was?" he asked.

"I am called Sharra."

"Sharra...a most unusual name. Well, Sharra, you will be safe from this Cestus here. And in return for the information you have furnished about an... enemy of Rome, I should like to display a measure of hospitality. You shall dine as my guest tonight."

"Thank you, my lord..." she began, but the prefect was already rising in dismissal, causing attendants to come rushing in from all sides, one to drape a cloak about his shoulders, another to proceed as path-clearer before him, and still another to bring up the rear.

That night, dining with the Roman officer in his private quarters, Sharra was attended by servants for the first time in her life. It was an experience as heady to her as the fine wine she was served, as delicious in its own way as the sumptuous food set before her, as thoroughly pleasing as the luxury and splendor of her surroundings. If this Roman lived in such a manner in what he disdainfully referred to in conversation as an outpost, how much more lavishly must he live at home? It was beyond her imagining for the moment, but she then and there decided it was something worth exploring.

Thus, regardless of what plans Marcellus Servianus might have had to lure her to his couch, she was already well ahead of him. And so, when that moment did arrive, when she had determined to her satisfaction that this young prince of Rome could summon the power to bring the mighty Cestus to his knees, she skillfully allowed herself to be seduced.

Much as she expected, the Roman's lovemaking was flabby and insipid compared to the tremors Cestus had caused within her.

But, of course, the Roman never suspected. Still basking in the afterglow of pleasure long after Sharra had departed his quarters, Marcellus Servianus reflected that no doubt this comely wench wanted something from him. But if all she desired was that he wield his authority to seek out and destroy the one she claimed had wronged her (which he surmised must indeed be her purpose), so much the better for them both. He would gladly grant her whatever vengeance she sought, never letting her know that it was she who was doing him the greater favor.

Because at long last he would rid himself of that galling specter from the past, would finally gain vengeance for being struck so viciously and openly by that slave boy.

XXVIII

In early spring the band began to wind its way down from the mountain heights. As they approached the region called Galilee, the sun traveled with them, warming their backs and calling forth new green grass to pad the paths of their horses. Good omens for a journey, though the clan needed no excuse, or even a destination, to break camp and go on the trail.

Cestus had suggested that he and the woman Rachel go alone. He would return soon, he had said. And though not one of the clan doubted his word, they all had been cooped up too long on the wintery heights. Besides, many of them were curious to see where this new woman had come from and what her people were like. And, more than one of the men wondered if she had any sisters that looked like her.

So they all set out together, traveling as was their custom with Cestus and his council up front, and the women and children spread out behind, with warriors traveling alongside and in the rear for protection, none of them save for the one woman in any hurry whatsoever. For the members of the clan of Cestus, it was the journey, not the destination that mattered.

Miriam, the sister of Zebediah, was at the well of Besara when she heard a familiar voice. She paused in the act of drawing water upward, reminded of a voice from another day (soft and small and musical as a bell) that used to call out "mother."

"Mother!"

The same voice again. Nearer now, more insistent.

Hesitantly, almost fearfully, she turned...and saw her daughter, Rachel, rushing toward her with outstretched arms.

Not until some minutes later, when the hugs and tears and tumble of words had subsided, did Miriam notice the large young man standing nearby, holding the reins of a horse. Cestus abided while a stream of relatives, friends, and those who were merely curious streamed in and out of Miriam's little house. The visitors were mostly women and mostly older, but there was one particular male, a sturdy-looking young man with skin darkened by exposure to the sun. He made a quiet entrance and stood waiting with no effort to push through the throng of bodies and chatter of voices, his eyes fastened on Rachel.

It was some time before her eyes found his. For a moment she stood open mouthed, then rushed toward him.

"Jarel!" she cried, holding out her arms.

"Rachel…" he murmured, entering her embrace. "Thank the Lord you are safe!"

They stood, locked arm in arm in a way that Cestus interpreted as being more like brother and sister than lovers.

"Is it true?" Rachel whispered when they parted. "Is Zebediah…?"

"Yes," Jarel answered softly.

"I…I can't believe that he is gone." Rachel wiped away a tear, and then took Jarel by the hand. "Come…I want you to meet someone."

That someone turned out to be a man young in years, with the most muscular frame Jarel had ever beheld.

"This is Cestus, the one who rescued me from the Romans," Rachel said. "And this," she said, turning to Cestus, "is Jarel…"

Before she could go on, Jarel extended a hand. "How can we ever thank you for returning Rachel to her home?"

Cestus extended a hand in return. "There is no need for thanks. Roman soldiers were chasing a young woman. I had no choice but to rescue her."

"Cestus speaks too modestly," Rachel said. "There were many Romans, and there was only Cestus and two of his men…and they destroyed all of the Romans."

"There was one Roman we spared," Cestus corrected.

"You spared one?" Jarel asked.

"Yes. He was wounded and could fight no longer."

Jarel was considering this when Rachel broke in. "Jarel is the one I spoke of who could tell you of Zebediah's words," she said to Cestus.

Cestus nodded. "I would like to hear of such things."

Jarel shook his head. "When Zebediah perished at the river, his words perished with him," he replied, his voice suddenly flat and empty.

When the last of the visitors had finally departed, Cestus took Rachel aside. "You and your mother must want to be alone to visit for a while, so I will go to let the clan know all is well," he told her. "I will come back for you in a three days, if you wish..." he finished in an uncharacteristically hesitant tone.

Rachel arched an eyebrow. "*If* I wish? Why would you think otherwise?"

"Well," he shrugged. "I thought that perhaps now that you are back among your family and your people, you might wish to stay..."

The eyebrow came down, and a soft smile lit up Rachel's face. "Of course I want you to come back for me. And if you don't," she teased, "I'll come looking for you!"

As he rode, Cestus considered again what he had determined to do. He had not told anyone, not even Rachel, but when he got back to where the clan members were encamped, he would tell them they must choose a new leader. It was not, he knew, a thing they would easily accept, but accept they must, for he had decided. When he returned to Rachel, he would put aside his old way of life and make a new life with her. Settle down in one place. Live in a house with walls and a roof. Put his skills to use in a trade that would provide for her...and for the family they would have.

So engrossed did he become in such thoughts that he found himself approaching a vaguely familiar incline without knowing quite how he had arrived there. He halted, suddenly very alert, for this seemed like the place where a sentry should be posted. But no one had hailed him.

Puzzled, for he could not believe that he had drifted very far off course no matter how preoccupied his thoughts, he urged his horse up the slope, muttering a string of curses for having let his mind wander. As he crested the hill, he saw that he was not lost after all, for the place of encampment was below. But there were no people. Or tents or horses.

His every sense on edge, he approached the deserted campsite. Everywhere there were signs of a hasty departure. He quickly picked up the trail and followed it, wondering what could have caused the clan to leave in such a fashion.

For the better part of an hour Cestus traced the flight of his people at a rapid pace. Then the trail narrowed and the signs grew fainter and fainter and disappeared altogether. He halted, considering what to do next, for even if his people had managed to escape whatever danger they had encountered, he might not be able to find them.

Let them go, a voice said. After all, that was what he was returning to the clan to do. Now the task had been taken off his hands. So let them go.

He looked about in desperation, searching for more than one answer. Some distance ahead a ridge jutted high above the landscape. He urged his horse toward it, seeking the vantage place of height. Just before he reached the top, he slid off his mount and crept forward on foot the last few yards, then peered cautiously over the rim.

At first glance he saw the dark form of a horse sprawled on the ground.

Beyond the horse, sunlight reflected from something pale and undefined.

Deep within him a drumbeat sounded. He mounted his horse and urged in carefully and made his way carefully down the slope, sweeping his eyes in all directions. A few feet from the carcass of the horse was a broken spear. He leaned down to examine it and recognized the steel head of a Roman pilum.

A horse dead that he had so often ridden beside...

The broken shaft of a Roman spear...

His people mysteriously scattered...

Above him the great circle of fire was searing the sky. Pushing through the thick haze of pulsating sunlight, he went racing toward the pale source of its reflection, the drumbeat sounding louder, and quicker, his breath erupting from his throat in a long, hoarse scream of denial.

Before him was a steep rise of hills with only a narrow fissure leading through to the other side. At the entrance to the pass, a rough, wooden cross had been thrust into the ground. Hanging from this terrible post, nailed through at the hands and feet, was the body of Malameus, the one who had been the first to join him.

Cestus halted before the torn and bloody lifeless form, then began to circle about it in rage and sorrow, raising his voice to the heavens as he paced, cursing the Romans for this thing they had done.

Every minute he delayed would make it that much harder to catch up with the others, if they still lived. Yet he could not allow the body of his comrade to stay out in the open in such a shameful display of death. Using his hands and his dagger, he hollowed out a shallow trench in the ground, then pried the torn body from the execution post, lowered it into the makeshift grave, and covered it as best he could with handfuls of thin, parched earth.

When he was finished, he tried to recall the prayers that were said over the dead of the people of his boyhood clan, but the words kept getting confused. Rachel, he thought; she would know how to pray. And which god to pray to. But he did not.

"This day you are free," he muttered at last. "This day you are truly free."

And then he was off, pushing through the narrow pass and beyond, racing the light of the sun. He knew that the people of the clan had come this way and that he must find them, yet the knowledge that he was leaving Rachel farther behind tormented him.

As the sun lowered toward the horizon, his horse began to labor. Cestus dismounted, drank from his water skin and then poured some into the weary animal's mouth. He started again on foot, giving his animal a rest from the burden of his weight.

A mile passed, then another, and a third. Sweat matted his hair and stung his eyes with salt; a terrible claw of pain closed about his chest and tightened until his torso bent low toward the ground; lances of fire pierced his thighs, searing them without mercy until the burning gave way to a blessed spreading numbness; then the numbness went away and the pain returned even worse than before, and this time it would not go away. He carried it with him on plodding legs into a barren stretch of land that he thought must be the end of the world. The sun fell away behind him, and he heard a voice saying that he was lost, and then another voice called his name aloud…

The people of the clan gathered together that night without a campfire, for the Romans might yet be nearby. But Cestus was with them, and so their courage was renewed.

After he had taken water and food, they told him how Malameus had discovered a Roman patrol and hurried back to camp with a warning. But the Romans caught the sounds of the camp being broken and came upon them, overtaking them on a narrow plain. Only the valiant one-man stand by Malameus at the pass had enabled the rest of the clan to escape.

"But why did the Romans not follow after they overcame Malameus?" Cestus wondered aloud.

Rolf, the third of the original triumvirate, shook his head uncertainly. "I waited at the far end of the pass, thinking that when the Romans came through, I would delay them awhile longer, but no Romans came. We could only guess that they were looking for you and thought they had found you in Malameus."

"Perhaps," Cestus replied in agreement.

"Even so, if it was you they were seeking, how could they have known our whereabouts?" someone questioned.

To this there was no answer.

That night Cestus lay awake debating within himself. He feared that if he was not there to lead them, his people would become an easy prey for their enemies, especially the Romans. On the other hand, Rachel should be safe for the time being among her own people. Had the Romans known she was in the town of Gedar, they would have gone there instead of the campsite. If it was Rachel they sought.

It would be best, then, he reasoned, trying to let his mind rule his heart, to take the clan to a distant place—lead them to safety and at the same time draw any pursuers away from Rachel.

Thus, despite his previous resolve, he rode again at the head of the clan, leading them in a quest to find a place beyond the reach of the Romans.

All that summer they wandered, and when the sun began to lose its power, they made a long camp. The hunters went out in force, and the women gathered the gifts that grew from the earth. And with the first hard falling of leaves, they were back on the move again.

Now they gradually wound their way up into the shelter of the highlands, retreating from the Romans and all other people until they arrived at a high, distant place where there was only the earth and the sky and the clan. And there they abided the long, bitter months of winter, apart from the rest of creation.

XXIX

Sharra often told herself that it was not such a bad life she had fallen into. Of course, this leader of the Romans was nothing like Cestus, but then neither was any other man.

She had quickly come to know more than a little about the Roman. He had not one name but three, and he had been sent from the great far-off city of Rome to assume a position of command at this place called Caesarea—a place which he obviously disliked but which to her was so wondrous that she could not even begin to imagine that the city from which the Romans took their name could be any larger or grander.

Yet though he held a position of power, he was not a warrior; he was not large or strong or, she was fairly certain, particularly brave. It might be that he was shrewd at tactics, she thought. One skilled in the strategy of war. More likely, she concluded, he was simply very rich and well connected.

But if the Romans chose such men as their leaders, how was it, she wondered, that Rome was in power throughout the world? Perhaps the soldiers who served under these leaders were very fierce fighters. Perhaps the Romans were so many in number that it simply did not matter who led them. Or perhaps this man with three names was the exception rather than the rule.

However it happened that he came to his position of power, this Roman was still much the same as any man. All of them were more alike than different. The strongest and most powerful among them could be made to bow before the weakness of a woman—if the woman knew how to turn that weakness to her advantage.

So she managed to put herself in the position of mistress to the rich Roman with three names. And if such a situation was not entirely to her liking, it did offer certain compensations. She enjoyed ease and comfort beyond anything she had ever dreamed of. Compared to the squalor she had known living in tents and huts of mud-caked settlements and facing the demands of some cruel and unwashed men who had claimed her body, she was living like a queen.

Still, there was that festering, galling torment, that thorn pressed deeply into the flesh of her mind that allowed her no rest: The slut Rachel still lived... and so did Cestus.

It had been surprisingly easy to persuade the Roman to dispatch troops in search of Cestus. Indeed, he had seemed eager to do her bidding in this regard. Nor had it been difficult to implant the idea that she should accompany the expedition to guide them in the right direction, though in truth she could only guess at the place where she had made her departure from the clan, let alone the path they had since taken. Still, the Roman scouts managed to find the encampment, but the clan caught wind of them and fled.

Bouncing alongside her benefactor in a chariot at the rear of the troops, Sharra had watched as the people of the clan raced across a tapering plain toward a pocket of hills. Just when it seemed the clan was trapped, they filtered through a cut in the rocks. A single warrior leaped from his horse and stationed himself before the narrow passageway. Though Sharra was unable to identify him because of the distance, she was sure it must be Cestus, for no one else would stand alone to face such a number of armed men.

For some time the solitary fighter held the Roman soldiers back, but at last sheer numbers overcame him. When this had been safely accomplished, Marcellus Servianus rode forth in triumph, accompanied by the woman.

Grasping the sides of the chariot with white-knuckled hands, Sharra held her breath against the moment she had brought about. As the chariot drew to a halt, she closed her eyes and braced herself. But when she dared to look at the body of the fallen warrior, it was not Cestus.

Dumbfounded, she cast her eyes about in furious inquiry. The band they had pursued was that of Cestus, for she recognized the dead man as one of the council. But where was the leader?

Though that question remained unanswered, two things were decided. One was that if Cestus had been with the clan, he would have been the one to stay and fight. The other was that there was no reason to pursue the clan if Cestus was not with them.

So that festering, galling torment not only remained but was magnified by a mystery added to it. Where was Cestus, if not with the clan?

Wherever he was, Sharra was determined to find him. And Rachel. So she continued to search on her own, using the resources that her relationship with Marcellus Servianus afforded to carefully spread the word that whoever delivered to her news of the whereabouts of the man and woman she sought would be richly rewarded. And whoever hid them would have no safe place to hide.

XXX

"It's all my fault," Miriam said, trying to sooth her weeping daughter as they sat outside the door to her little house. "If only I hadn't listened to that silly dream and brought you to Zebediah."

"No, don't blame yourself," Rachel replied. "It wasn't a silly dream; it was a vision. A vision, mother, so there must be a reason for all that has happened."

"What reason could there be for such terrible things? Zebediah was slain. And so were many others. And you...you were taken hostage by the Romans."

"Yes, but Cestus rescued me. I always felt that was the reason for all that had happened: to bring the two of us together. But now, now that he has not returned, I fear something terrible has happened." Rachel paused to wipe away a tear. "You know, I didn't even have to ask him to bring me here to see you. It seemed he just knew what was in my heart and so he offered. He even said that he wished to hear the words of Zebediah from those who knew him. But now I don't know. I just don't know, mother..."

Miriam shook her head sadly. "I have come to think that it might have been better off if such words had never been spoken."

"No, mother. Please don't say that."

"Well, look at what has come of his words. They were the death of him. And of others who followed him. Look at what has become of Jarel..."

Rachel lowered her eyes. "Truly he is not the same Jarel I once knew. He seems so...so pale. In both body and spirit."

"Jarel's spirit perished that day at the river," Miriam said. "He told me not long after he returned how my brother's words had given meaning to his life, but now he feared those words were as rainbows painted in the sky. Here but for a brief moment in time. Then he said perhaps it was better to just accept things the way they are, they way they are and always will be."

"But still, now he has gone in search of one that some say is the true Messiah," Rachel protested. "The Teacher from Nazareth."

"Hah! Jarel has been gone for nearly a month now. Who knows if he will ever come back? Besides, what good has ever come from Nazareth?" Miriam let out a long sigh. "Ah, well, what is done is done. Right now, it is time for me to start preparing supper. Sit awhile longer. I'll call you if I need help."

Miriam gave her daughter a hug, and then rose to her feet. "He will come back, you know," she said. "This young man of yours. He cares for you deeply. You can see it in his eyes."

Rachel watched her mother disappear through the doorway, then leaned back and closed her eyes. And for the first time in days, a smile gradually eased across her worried face.

He will come back, she had said.

He will come back…

"Rachel…"

She looked up with a start, for she had not heard anyone approach, and then scrambled to her feet. "Jarel!"

"I saw him! I saw him and I heard him!" Jarel said, his words tumbling out of his mouth so rapidly they tripped over his tongue. "I followed the Word, and just beyond the southern shore of the great lake I saw a crowd gathering. And there he was, standing on a hillside. He…" Jarel held his hands out before him as if trying to conjure up an image out of the air so that Rachel might see what he had. "He is much younger than Zebediah was. And larger in stature, though he seems gentle in manner, as was our master. But his voice! Ah…" He shook his head in wonder. "You should hear his voice! Even if there are a thousand people gathered, somehow it seems as if he is speaking to you alone."

"I saw him more than once," he went on. "I followed along behind him and the ones called his disciples. He has the power to perform miracles. He heals the sick and lame, he causes the blind to see, he casts out demons…" Here he paused and fixed Rachel with a piercing, desperate gaze, seeking to somehow transfer from his mind to hers all that he had seen and heard. "You must hear his words," he rasped. "Truly the things he speaks are not of this world."

Miriam had heard Jarel's voice and hurried outside. Now she moved to his side and touched his arm solicitously, hoping to calm him, for he seemed dangerously overwrought. "Come inside and rest," she said. "I will bring you some wine…"

Jarel nodded absently but did not move.

"It is said he comes from Nazareth," he said. "How strange…how strange that he was among us all this time…"

"What do you mean?" Rachel asked.

"I mean that the prophecy has been fulfilled," he said, his eyes glowing with excitement. "The one Zebediah foretold is here. The Messiah walks among us!"

XXXI

Cestus arose from his place of sleeping without having slept, gathered his weapons and belongings, and quietly folded his tent.

The decision had not been easy. Besides harboring a strong sense of responsibility for his people, he had deep feelings of respect and affection for many of them as well. They had become his family.

Still, it was a thing that had to be done, for between the woman and the clan the choice was clear in his heart, if not his mind.

The evening before, he had faced his people and told them of his decision. At a feast held in his honor, he had clasped his comrades one by one and bid them farewell. Now, in the cool, soft shadows of the hour that hung between the old day and the new, he mounted his horse and rode out of the encampment.

Rachel made her way outside on soft footsteps to say her morning prayers. It looked like it was going to be a warm and sunny day. And with that thought, tears welled up unbidden in her eyes, for it was on just such a day that she and Cestus had begun the trip down from the mountain heights, a journey that had left her alone in her mother's house and him gone to some unknown place, never to return.

Her eyes blurred, so the slanting rays of first light appeared to come from beneath the sea, and she shut them altogether and put her head down in her hands.

"Why are you crying?"

Startled, for she had not realized that Miriam was up and about, she quickly dabbed at her eyes, trying to think of a quick and simple answer that would forestall any further inquiry. Then it occurred to her that the voice was not that of her mother.

Drawing in her breath, she whirled about.

In one swift movement, he stepped forward and swept her up in his arms.

When her feet touched the ground again, she looked up at him through tears of joy and wonder.

"Is it you?" she said. "Is it really, really you?"

"Yes. Yes, of course it is…"

"Then hold me! Hold me…and don't ever let me go!"

"Never," he said, holding her close to his chest. "Never again."

Safely wrapped within Cestus's strong arms, Rachel, closed her eyes, feeling his heart beat s against her own chest.

Neither Rachel nor Cestus noticed that Miriam, awakened by the sound of voices, and the soft neighing of a horse, had gotten out of bed and come to the door. Seeing Cestus, Miriam stopped short. Her hand went to her breast and her mouth hung open, but she said nothing. Instead, she retreated just inside the door.

"What happened? Rachel asked after awhile. "When you didn't come back I feared something terrible had happened. Or…"she hesitated "….or that you had changed your mind. That you didn't…didn't want me anymore and so you just rode away."

"No!" Cestus leaned back and looked directly into her eyes. "The truth is, I had made up my mind to go back to the clan and tell them they must find a new leader. That I was going to return to you and make a life with you among your people." Then he told her of returning to the campsite to find his clan scattered, of following the dwindling trail, discovering the body of Malameus, and eventually coming upon the clan just before nightfall.

"That night I had a terrible choice to make," he went on. "Lead my people to safety or return to you. I chose to lead the clan because the Romans were searching for me and if I returned to your village I might put you in danger. So I led my people to the mountains but the harsh winter trapped us there. When the winter finally passed I told the clan they must choose a new leader for I was going to return to you. And that if you would have me, I would stay with you in your village, or anywhere else you choose. And so, here I am."

"If I would have you? There is no if! Every hour of every day since you have been gone I have prayed for you, longed for you…"

Unable to keep silent any longer, Miriam stepped out of the doorway. "I told you he would come back," she said to Rachel, smiling with the words. Then, turning to Cestus, "Thanks be to the Lord our God for brining you safely back to us. Please, come inside and refresh yourself."

As they ate bread and fruit and cheese, Cestus repeated to Miriam, who never let on that she had already heard, much of what he had told Rachel. "From this day forward I will wander no more," he concluded. "I can build a sturdy house for us. I have coins from when I was among the Romans and I can do any kind of work that is to be done. And, I want to become part of the family of your village. Rachel and I were wed according to the custom of my clan, but we should also become man and wife according to the tradition of your people."

At this Miriam bowed her head for a moment. When she raised up again her voice was soft with joy. "I know a place where you can stay," she said.

It turned out that Jarel had left indefinitely to follow after the new prophet and had given his house to Miriam to look after. That very day Cestus set about getting the house in order. He put his expertise with fashioning weapons to use making tools to use in his work and by the end of the first full month he had repaired the roof, shored up a cracked wall and generally cleaned up the place and its surroundings. He had also amassed a growing audience of men of the village who were interested in his ability to make tools and awed by his enormous strength and endurance.

During this time the relatives of Miriam made preparations for the upcoming marriage. On the appointed day Rachel was dressed in a gown, a sash was put around her waist, and her eyes were covered with a veil. Then, accompanied by family and friends, she proceeded to the home of Cestus. There the groom came out to meet her, removed the veil, unfastened the sash, and led her inside. The similarities of this simple ceremony, though somewhat more elaborate, to that of the clan of Cestus was not lost on either the bride nor the groom.

Rachel knew, but she waited until the third moon before she shared the secret with her beloved. He was tending to his weapons, sharpening his sword and fashioning new arrows. She watched for a few moments, even yet unsure how to tell him, then sat down by his side.

"I have something to tell you," she began.

Cestus stopped what he was doing and gave her his full attention.

"I…you…I mean, we…are going to have a baby. A son."

When the mighty and fearless warrior regained breath enough to speak, he asked how she could be so certain the baby would be a boy.

"I just know," she said with an enigmatic smile. "I just know."

Now that she was with child, Rachel woke up every morning giving thanks for the blessings the Lord had bestowed upon her. Still, blessed as she was, there was one thing she wished for, though she found it hard to understand.

Finally, before it would be too late, she asked if they might make a small journey.

Just as she suspected, once she assured him it was safe for her to travel, but that they must go soon, before she became too heavy with child, he had no objection. Though he had not spoken of it, his spirit was already chafing at being confined within so many walls. If going in search of this teacher Rachel spoke of meant mounting his horse and heading out along an open trail, then it was a thing to be done.

Rachel had word of where the one she sought might be found, but even without guidance, the way would have been clear. There were scarcely out of sight of Gedar when the main road began to clog with people. And before they traveled the distance of another hour, the seekers had become so many that the dust and clamor of their passing could be seen and heard for well over a mile in any direction. It was strange, Cestus thought, guiding his horse out away from the plodding multitude, that so great a number of people would venture forth not to see men fight in in the arena or women dance or magicians conjure but only to hear a man speak. Whoever this man was, he must have great powers.

As the procession approached a small cover outside of the town of Capernaum, someone shouted, "There he is!"

At the distance from which Cestus first beheld the man named Jesus, he could see nothing unusual about him. Perhaps when he got closer, Cestus thought, he would discover the source of this teacher's power. Then Jesus began to speak, and after the first few words, Cestus realized that though he was at the farthest reaches of the crowd, he could hear as if he was but an arm's length away.

Much of what Cestus heard was framed in parables, and he had to search for meaning. The kingdom of God was at hand, the teacher proclaimed, but it was not a kingdom of earthly principalities and earthly power. Rather it was a kingdom of love, and it was hidden within the hearts of men. And when love was set free therein, then all would be free.

Free!

It was a word of many shapes of meanings, Cestus told himself. A word that men often bent to their own advantage. Yet much of what he was hearing he was able to see through Rachel.

That before the power of love, the desires of self could be set aside.

That where love dwelled, no man could make a slave of any other man, or woman.

That where there was love, there was in like measure an absence of fear and hatred and greed and violence, an absence of all the many mad cravings that kept men locked in chains of their own forging.

He heard many other things, all of which were strange to his ears.

How the poor and the downtrodden would someday be exalted.

How you must relinquish the things of the world before you could possess those of the kingdom.

And something else, something that inexplicably transported Cestus back to the hillside of his childhood where he used to look with wonder and awe at the great, immeasurable night sky: I am the Light and the Way. Whoever follows after me does not awaken unto darkness, but unto the light of life everlasting.

Then Jesus finished and began to move with his disciples through the crowd, and Cestus wondered if indeed he had truly heard the things burning within his mind, for he felt as if he was emerging from a long and deep slumber. Then something happened that caused him to wonder all the more.

"I can see! I can see!" a voice cried out. "Praise you, Master! I can see!"

A young man in ragged clothes was dancing about, holding his hands up in front of his eyes. "I can see!" he kept exclaiming. "My eyes have been opened!"

"He has been blind since childhood!" another man declared loudly. "But the Master has healed him! He put a single finger to each eye, and his sight was restored!"

At first Cestus thought that it must be some kind of trick, some sham or deceit. And with that thought came an angry sense of disappointment, for until then the words he had heard had seemed free of the mud and dust of the world.

But others spoke up who knew the youth and had witnessed the miracle. Though their voices were jumbled with excitement, their stories were much the same: the young man had been guided into the path of Jesus, and there he had knelt, beseeching the Master to have pity. Jesus had halted and looked down upon the petitioner, then raised his face toward the heavens. When he looked down again, he placed a finger on each of the blind man's eyes.

And immediately the blind man could see.

The disciples of Jesus were clearing a path through the crowd, and Cestus was seized by a sudden fear—though he could not say why or even why it should matter—that he would never see this man of mystery again. He was starting to nudge his mount forward when Jesus turned and swept his gaze over the crowd until it came to rest directly upon him. For a brief but timeless moment, Cestus found himself locked into eyes that were a window to another world, and in that instant he heard a voice proclaim, "A gift far greater than this awaits you."

Then Jesus continued on his way.

Cestus pondered within himself until they had distanced themselves from most of the crowd before turning to Rachel. "What do you think he meant?" he asked.

"Meant when?" Rachel asked, still dazzled by all she had seen and heard. Zebediah had been a holy man. A prophet. But this Jesus of Nazareth was something beyond even that. Perhaps Jarel was right. Perhaps he *was* the Messiah.

"Just before he departed. I heard the words so clearly, but what did he mean?"

"What were these words?"

"Don't you remember? He looked at me and said, 'A gift far greater than this awaits you.'"

"I heard no such words," Rachel said, her brow furrowed.

"But...I heard him so plainly, just as if he was standing by my side..." Cestus let his voice trail off. Rachel's eyes were fixed upon him, searching and puzzled. Somehow, what Jesus said had not reached her ears, but how could that be? His voice had been so clear.

They had moved only a short distance from the cove when Rachel felt a wave of nausea sweeping over her. It was just the heat of the day, she reassured herself. That and the press of so many people. A second wave came, stronger than the first, causing her to tremble before a dark foreboding that travel on horseback might somehow have harmed her unborn child.

Cestus felt her grip tighten at his waist. Turning, he saw that her face looked drained of blood. "Are you all right?" he asked, bringing the horse to a halt.

"I'm...just a little tired," she said. "Perhaps we could rest for a while..."

The only shelter in sight was a thin bundle of trees. Cestus guided the horse to the trees and spread out a blanket for Rachel to recline on. By the time she had taken a few sips of water, the color had already returned to her cheeks.

"I'm all right. Truly, I'm fine now," she said reassuringly, for the face of her beloved was wrinkled with worry. "It was only your son, making his presence known."

Cestus nodded, visibly relieved, but stayed close by her side, fanning away the heat and the flies that were buzzing about like a swarm of tiny buzzards. "You should eat something," he said. And when she nodded assent, he got up and went to his horse to unpack the food they had brought for the midday meal.

He was standing there beside his horse, lost in visions of Rachel and their unborn child, when a faint but unmistakable cadence of footsteps brought him to full alert.

Romans!

At first his mind refused to accept what his ears were reporting, but when he looked in the direction of the sound, he saw a column of soldiers coming up the road, moving with speed and precision. When they came to the little stand of trees, they formed a crisp and orderly line, and one of them stepped forward.

"We seek the one called Cestus!" he called out.

Cestus wondered how they had managed to find him here, and why, but this was not the time for questions and answers. Quickly surveying the soldiers, he counted eight foot soldiers and two horsemen. "I am Cestus," he said. "A free man."

At this an officer on horseback moved out from behind the ranks. "I am in command here," the officer declared. "And I pronounce your free status forfeit by reason of crimes committed against Imperial Rome. Therefore, Cestus, throw down your weapons and surrender!"

There was something disturbingly familiar about this Roman on horseback, something Cestus could not quite put his finger on.

"Do you not recognize your master? Then look more closely, slave!" the officer taunted, removing his helmet.

Marcellus Servianus! The sight of him left Cestus dumbfounded. How could it be that this son of a rich Roman could be here, in this far distant land? And at the head of a column of soldiers?

"I know that one," Rachel said, her voice barely a whisper.

"So do I," he said quietly, keeping his unblinking eyes fixed on the enemy.

"We Romans are civilized people," Marcellus Servianus was saying. "Surrender peacefully and your lives will be spared. When I give the signal, my centurion will begin counting. If you do not lay down your weapons by the time he reaches the number ten, the blood of you both will be on your own hands."

For a moment Cestus considered laying down his arms, but if he did the Romans would either kill them both or cast them into a life of slavery.

The centurion was counting, marking off the numbers crisply.

The beast within rattled its cage, clamoring to be loosened.

"There are so many of them," Rachel said hoarsely, her voice constricted with fear. "What are we going to do?"

"Kill them!" Cestus answered, springing up into the saddle.

"Don't be a fool!" Marcellus Servianus shouted. "We have you outnumbered by ten to one!"

"You should have brought more!" Cestus shot back. Notching an arrow into his bow, he let out a roar of such terrible fury that the horse of the Roman commander reared up and dumped its rider unceremoniously to the ground.

Among the legionaries chosen for the mission were hardened veterans, but none of them had ever encountered anything like the berserker raging against them. Arrows came hurtling as from the very mouth of the warhorse, cutting down half of the first unit. And then the terrible sword went seeking.

Stunned by the fall, Marcellus Servianus groped awkwardly to his feet. Through the choking haze of dust he saw shadowy figures scrambling about in panic. He reached for his horse and commanded it to stand still, but totally disregarding the rank and station of its rider, it turned and galloped away. As he stood there screaming at the disappearing horse, Marcellus heard another thundering of hoofs. Turning, he saw the dark form of the demon's stallion bearing down upon him. He let out a strangled cry, threw up his arms as if to ward off the galloping monster…and collapsed in a faint.

Cestus lifted his horse up and over the prostate form, and then wheeled quickly about. Behind him bodies lay dead and broken along the swift alley of his destruction. The centurion had been among the first to fall, and without someone to rally them, the troops were scattering. At the fringe of it all, three of them were heading toward Rachel.

Kicking urgently at his horse, Cestus went racing in their direction. He quickly overtook the nearest two and sent them into the afterworld minus their heads. The third, seeing what had happened to his comrades, veered off and ran for his life, and Cestus let him keep it.

Reigning in alongside Rachel, Cestus gathered her up into the saddle, and at her touch the beast within subsided. "You are safe now," he told her. "It is all right. You are safe…"

The soldier that Cestus had spared stumbled and fell. And as he regained his feet, he looked back in terror, expecting to see the sword of death swooping down upon him. Instead he saw that the ferocious warrior had turned aside for the woman. Scarcely able to believe his luck, the soldier began to back quickly away, but his feet got entangled in dust and dread and he went tumbling to the ground a second time.

Cursing, he scrambled up again and saw that the warrior had lifted the woman atop his horse and that his back was turned. The soldier considered, hesitated, then hefted his spear and crept a couple of paces forward, keeping low to the ground. After a few more steps, he decided he was temporarily invisible and straightened up and went running toward the pair. Gathering momentum, he took careful aim and hurled the spear with all his might.

Rachel wrapped her arms about the neck of her beloved Cestus and rested her head on his chest. They must go, he was saying, his heartbeat strong in her ear. She loosened her hold and shifted about to sit behind him on the horse, and as she did so something struck her from behind.

Stunned, she opened her mouth to speak, but there seemed to be no air in her lungs. She tried again, felt the horse sliding away beneath her, and a thick, warm flow of liquid spilled out over her silent words.

XXXII

Rachel died at sunset, in a barren mountain pass unmarked on any map. There was nothing Cestus could do to save her. The spear had penetrated deeply, and to a vital spot. Though she lived for several hours after, she only regained consciousness once. She opened her eyes and looked searchingly about, and when she saw Cestus, she smiled. Then she sighed deeply, closed her eyes, and lived no more.

At the moment of her death, the great warrior threw back his head and let out a searing wail of pain and loss and sorrow. And then he wept. In the solitude of that most lonely and bitter of nights he mourned, and when he was at last dry of tears, he paced about in furious unquenchable anguish, hurling questions for which there were no answers at the dark night sky.

No-thought would not serve him then, nor would anything else he had learned in all the hard years of his life. Of the few things on earth he had found to be good, Rachel was by far the best. Now she had been taken from him, and nothing else mattered, not even himself.

When dawn came he went out and began hacking at scrub trees and saplings, fashioning thin poles, which he lashed together to form a crude coffin. When it was finished, he very carefully, very gently, very tenderly, placed Rachel's body inside and fastened the lid tightly. But instead of burying the earth-sprung sarcophagus, he affixed it to long poles, which he attached to either side of his saddle so he could pull it along behind him.

All that day he rode, keeping a tight rein on the horse, tormented anew with every anxious backward glance. That night he kept a vigil beside Rachel's body. And when at last he fell asleep, he dreamed she was alive and well, and in dreaming he smiled. But when he awoke, it was to that other, sadder dream, and there all smiles had died.

The new day came upon the land as if from a furnace, and with each passing hour the heat became more intense. The odor of death rode with him now, but Cestus tried to deny its presence. He had seen much of killing and dying, and he recognized the inescapable finality of it all. Yet even though he had seen Rachel die with his own eyes, so overwhelming was his grief, so tortured his mind, that he harbored the desperate idea that she was merely under a spell. And when the spell was broken, she would awaken before him, full of life and joy and beauty.

As the sun climbed to noon in the sky, the heat of the day seemed unbearably fierce; his mouth was dry, his tongue was swollen, and his body was drenched with sweat. He halted to rest his horse and dismounted to look again upon the altar of the roughhewn casket, his pulse thudding dully at his temple.

Visions of Rachel filled his head to bursting. Inside the box she laid waiting, her skin soft and smooth, her dark eyes shining, her lips parted in a smile.

Once more…just once more…he had to gaze upon her unparalleled beauty.

With trembling hands he grasped the lid and ripped it loose…and fell back with a terrible, stricken cry.

Retching and gasping and heaving, tears streaming down his anguished face, he crawled away from the terrible box on his hands and knees. For in it he had beheld not the warm, lush beauty of the Rachel he had known, but a steaming, maggot-infested corpse, a thing of horror spewed up from the underworld.

It took all of his courage to approach the monstrosity of the makeshift coffin again, but it was a thing that had to be done. When the task was finished, he retreated to the uppermost heights, far away from the raw wound of the shallow grave. There he gathered his strength, stoking his rage for the day he would begin his quest.

His plan was simple.

He was going to kill the Romans.

He would seek them out, singly or in groups. Kill them and take their weapons and supplies. Free their slaves along the way, so that as his victories grew, so would his force. In time he would forge a great army. And when this was accomplished, there would be no more slaves, but only free people. But strangely enough, when he wound his way back down the mountain in search of the Romans, he found not a one. Day after day he made his way without encountering a single human being, Roman or otherwise.

It was as if a gigantic unseen hand had wiped all other people off the earth, swept them to some dark and hidden place along with his beloved Rachel.

The daylight hours became unbearably lonely, but the nights were a far greater ordeal. Sleep became harder and harder, and one night Cestus found himself watching the stars and thinking of the long-ago nights when he had sat outside his father's tent and looked in awe at those same tiny, glowing lights. What were they? he wondered again, much as he had wondered as a child. And why were they? The years had brought him many things, but seldom any answers.

As always, his thoughts turned to Rachel. When they had been together, the nights were warm and filled with light. If only he could have her back, he would tell her this. He would hold her in his arms and tell her this and all the many things he should have told her but somehow had left unsaid.

When at last he slept, it was a troubled sleep, riddled with strange and disturbing dreams. He awakened with the rising sun. And as his eyes opened, he saw her. She came walking into his campsite with the sun at her back so that she seemed to be emerging from a great halo of light. For a moment he stared in disbelief, and then he saw that it was truly her. Really and truly her! He jumped to his feet and started toward her, his heart leaping out before him.

"Cestus…" she called. And at the sound of her voice he tried to hurry even more, but some unseen force held him back. He dug his feet into the ground and pushed with all his might, but no matter how hard he tried, he could not move.

"Go to Besara," she said, and now Cestus thought he saw another figure, shadowy and indistinct, appear behind her. "There Jarel will be waiting."

Then she was gone. She did not turn and walk away, she simply vanished. Cestus looked frantically about, now fully awake and able to move. Could it have been just another dream? Some trick of the mind? Falling to his knees, he began to beat on the ground with his fists, trying to pound away the festering torment that would not give him ease even in sleep. It had been so real! She had stood there, not ten paces away! And she had spoken! He had seen her and heard her and she had been real!

Over and over again he hammered at the unyielding earth, pounding until his mighty hands were aching and his lungs were empty of breath. At last, beginning to despair of his sanity, he rose unsteadily to his feet and made ready to break camp. Perhaps it was all just a dream, but he would go to Besara to find out.

At every leg of the journey, he told himself he was a fool for following a dream. Worse than a fool, he was a madman to think that Jarel would actually be waiting for him. But when he at last arrived at Besara, there Jarel was, standing just outside the gates of the city.

"Peace be with you," he called out, apparently not at all surprised to see Cestus.

Cestus dismounted and walked slowly toward Jarel, wondering if he was in another dream. "How was it you happened to be here just now?" he asked. "Outside the city gates…"

"I was waiting for you."

Only on the rarest of occasions did Jarel take so much as even a single cup of wine, but as he listened to the story of how Rachel had been killed in the Roman ambush, he consumed the better part of a flask. When Cestus was finished there was a heavy silence.

"You could not have heard," Jarel said at last, "but while you were gone, Miriam passed away." Then he reached for the flask again and by the time the first stars appeared in the night sky, he was dead to the world.

On the other hand, Cestus was so overwrought that no matter how much wine he consumed, he was unable to even approach sleep. So when his temporary drinking companion retired, he grabbed a wineskin in one hand and his sword in the other and stumbled outside.

As he made his way, he vowed that on the morrow he would begin again his quest for vengeance. This much he had to do, for no one else would—not her family, not the men of her village, not her long-winded prophets…not even her almighty god.

At the thought of the god Rachel had so often spoken of, Cestus began to pace about in agitation. God! He snarled the word in derision. The one true god, Rachel had said. A god of endless love and mercy. And what love and mercy did this god show to Rachel? What protection did he offer? Tell me, god that no one can see, he silently raged, why did you take the life of Rachel? Answer me—if you exist!

Tossing the wineskin aside, he grasped the hilt of his sword with both hands, raised it above his head, and plunged the blade into the ground.

Why? he demanded, pushing the blade deeper into the earth. Why? Why? Why? But of course there was no answer. Just as there was no god, he told himself, but only a bunch of statues and carvings of things that men had made up in their minds.

He let loose of his earth-entrenched sword and leaned back against the trunk of a tree and closed his eyes, wishing he could shut off all the questions and raging and sorrow and fall into the soft arms of sleep.

"Steppan..."

Cestus sat up quickly, surprised that he had not heard anyone approach. A man was standing before him, clothed in a cloak and hood that obscured his face.

"Do not trouble yourself to rise," the man said. "I come in peace."

Confident of his own powers, Cestus settled back down against the tree, concerned more that the man might have seen him weeping than for any threat against his person.

"Steppan," the man said again, and it dawned on Cestus that the stranger had called him by the name given him at birth, "it is time to kill the beast in order that the man might live."

With these words the speaker raised his hands. And even by the pale light of the moon, Cestus could plainly see the marks of wounds.

"Behold..." the voice continued, and now Cestus recognized it, and with that recognition came an overwhelming urge to pull back the hood and gaze upon that hidden countenance, but his body was not in his control. "A gift has been promised you, and now it is delivered. Go forth and bear witness to all men, Steppan, that the cross has power over the sword."

Cestus felt his eyes being pulled toward his sword as if his head was attached to a string. Thrust into the ground just beyond his feet, the blade and hilt of the terrible instrument of death formed the dark outline of a cross. A light came forth from the hand of the speaker and touched the sword. And as it did so, the blade broke in half and the hilt fell to the ground.

At that exact moment, a searing pain ripped through Cestus's chest, causing him to double over in agony. Then, as brief as it was excruciating, it was gone. Cestus uncoiled himself slowly, probing his body for a wound, but the pain had come from within. Dumbfounded, he looked toward the source of the magical light, his mouth forming a thousand questions.

But the man was gone.

Whatever it was he had experienced, the shattered sword was proof to Cestus that it had not been a dream. Leaving the sword in place, he ran back to the house.

"Jarel!" he shouted. "Wake up!"

Jarel mumbled something unintelligible, trying to rouse himself from the depths of wine-induced first sleep.

"Come on!" Cestus shook him by the shoulders. "Wake up! I just saw the Teacher. The one Rachel took me to see. The one called Jesus. I just saw him!"

Jarel sat up. "Where?" he asked, suddenly awake.

"Just outside. I was sitting beneath a tree when he suddenly appeared. He called me by my given name of Steppan, and…"

Jarel reached for a candle and lit it. "Are you certain it was the one named Jesus?" he said, reminding himself that it was late and Cestus had been drinking. "You only saw him once."

"It was his voice. I recognized him by his voice. It was the same man, Jarel! But there were marks at his hands and wrists. Deep, open wounds."

The candle dropped from Jarel's hand and lay sputtering on the floor. "Lord!" he whispered, looking at Cestus with a mixture of awe and bewilderment.

Cestus stooped to pick up the candle and handed it to Jarel. "What?" he asked.

"Have you not heard?"

"Heard what?"

"That Jesus of Nazareth was crucified."

"But…that cannot be," Cestus protested. "I saw him just now."

"Yes…yes, I believe you did, Cestus. For the story of Jesus does not end with the cross. You see, after he died and was buried, he rose up from out of the tomb."

Cestus stared at Jarel in bewilderment, unable to comprehend the strange things that were taking place all about him. "Have you, yourself, seen him after the cross?" he asked, seeking not so much verification of the tale of resurrection as of his own sanity.

"I have," Jarel answered. "It was he who told me to await you outside the city gates."

XXXIII

Jarel had observed Cestus closely, had questioned and probed, had even stood over him watching while he was asleep. In appearance he was the same, but in spirit he seemed truly a new man. A man reborn. To Jarel it was another great mystery, yet at the same time proof in the flesh of that for which he had so long been seeking.

The morning after Cestus's vision, Jarel began to relate to him all that he knew of Jesus: his teachings, his miracles, his trial and execution on the cross... and his resurrection from the tomb. Everything that Cestus heard filled him with wonder—and with questions burning for answers.

...If Jesus was the road to eternal life, what about all those people who had lived before he came to dwell on earth? Or who lived in places where his word did not reach? What about his father and mother? How could anyone be condemned for not accepting something they did not know about?

...Could it be that God had sent other sons, in other times and places, so that those people could know and be saved? Still, how could it be that if God so loved the world that he sent his son to die for the salvation of the beings who inhabited the world that so many were allowed to perish unsaved?

There were so many questions, so many mysteries, but of this Cestus was sure: his sword had been shattered, and he had been given a message to deliver. So he continued to question, and listen, and ponder within himself.

"So Jesus went willing to the cross, even though he was the son of God?" he asked Jarel.

"He went *because* he was the son of God," Jarel answered. "That was his mission. He suffered death so that all mankind might have life. His blood was the ransom for our sins, the sacrifice by which we have been redeemed."

"But he must have known he would come back to life, if he was the son of God."

"I cannot say. Jesus was…was God-become-man. Thus, the part of him that was man must have feared and doubted just like any other man. But it is all a great mystery. A very great mystery. And I am not a wise man, Cestus, just one who believes."

"No, Jarel, you *are* a wise man, because you know there are things you do not know."

Jarel laughed. "I think *you* are the wise one."

"I have been called many things," Cestus said, laughing in return, "but never wise." He was quiet for some time, trying to digest all he was hearing. Then he spoke up with yet another question. "So, tell me, what exactly did Jesus say a man must do to have eternal life?"

"Jesus said the key is love—love for the Lord God and love for your fellow man."

"Love even for your enemy?"

"Especially for your enemy. Because where there is love there can be no fear, and where there is no fear there is no hatred or anger or violence. And when these things have died, all humankind will live in peace and harmony."

"That I can see," Cestus said. Then he came out with what for him was *the* question: Why had God allowed Rachel to die? To be killed when she was so young, and with child. Why had God allowed both mother and child, his child, his son, to die?

Here Jarel paused for some time before replying. "It may be," he said softly, "that as horrible as it was, her death was the instrument of your salvation—and the salvation of others. Only God knows, but had you stayed on the life path you were on, you soul might never had been saved, and so you would not have been able to save others. All things of this world pass away, Cestus. So we must divest ourselves of the things of this world, and prepare for the world to come. That, I think, was the message. But know this: Rachel's body has died, but her spirit still lives. And I believe, I truly believe, that you will be joined with her again."

The questions kept coming so thick and fast that Jarel suggested they go down to Jerusalem to meet with the followers of Jesus who had heard his words and seen his deeds.

On the morning of their departure, Jarel arose to find the house empty. Puzzled, for the new day was still cloaked in shadows, he made his way outdoors. And there he saw Cestus, kneeling beside the tree where his sword had been shattered. Thinking that he was praying, Jarel did not disturb him. Then Cestus arose. And as he turned, Jarel saw what he had been doing. Around his neck was a leather cord. Attached to the cord was the hilt of the broken sword. Hanging down about his chest, it formed a heavy symbol of the cross.

So it was that, much as Lucius Portius had heard, the man called Cestus, barbarian, slave, gladiator, warrior chieftain, a man whose very name was the drumbeat of death, joined the followers of a man from Nazareth named Jesus, who had been crucified for the words he spoke about love and everlasting life.

XXXIV

"Are you ready?" Jarel asked.

Cestus nodded, unable for the moment to utter a word. They had spent some time with the brothers in Jerusalem, and after a period of questioning and being questioned, Cestus had plunged once again beneath the surface of a river of water. But this time he was seeking not an end to life but a life without end.

The morning after his baptism, he and Jarel set about their mission. By midafternoon they came upon a group of men gathered in discussion at the marketplace of a small village. After listening for a while, Jarel wormed his way to the forefront and waited until all eyes were upon him.

"My name is Jarel," he began. "I come from Gedar, in Galilee. I was a follower of the prophet Zebediah," at this there was a murmur of recognition, "and in more recent times of Jesus of Nazareth. A friend is with me today. His name is Steppan," he said, using the given name of his friend rather than the Roman name. "He has come from a far distant land, and I ask you spare a few minutes to listen to his words." Every eye turned to the one who had been introduced, but he stood there as if made of stone. All his life he had been a man of action, not words. Now that he had to rely on the power of his tongue instead of his arm, he felt completely unarmed. A sudden panic rose within him that in its own way was as strong as any he had experienced before stepping onto the sands of death. How would he find the words to tell these strangers of the mystery that was as far beyond his understanding as were the stars of his childhood nights?

Throats were cleared, feet began to shuffle, a low murmur ran through the assembly, and still he said nothing. Jarel had assured him that the Spirit that had set him on this mission would give him the words to fulfill it, but nothing was coming out of his mouth.

"What is that thing about your neck?" someone questioned.

"This is…this was…my sword," Cestus said. Having managed those words, he began to tell his story, going back to the time when he had been captured as a boy and sold into slavery. But as he spoke, one by one, and then in groups, the men of the assembly turned their backs to his words and went on their way.

As the last of them made their exit, Cestus looked despairingly toward Jarel.

"It's all right," Jarel said reassuringly. "We must take this as a sign that you have been given a great work to do, and thus Satan will oppose you. The next time will be better, Cestus. Each time it will go better."

Jarel's assurances turned out to be wishful thinking. Time and time again, a similar chain of events was repeated. Jarel would step before an assembly and ask that a friend be allowed to speak. But at the very outset that friend had been identified as Cestus, a gladiator of Rome and a warrior chieftain. A killer of men. Word of this spread quickly through the community and closed ears and hearts to his words.

Rather than make any attempt to hide his past, Cestus openly confessed it. All that he had been was, he declared, the very reason he had been chosen to spread the Word.

"I was the worst sinner of all," he would proclaim. "Yet Jesus redeemed me from my sins. By his sacrifice on the cross, he rescued my soul. Mine and yours and all of humanity! I stand before you to bear witness that the power of the cross is greater than that of the sword. Behold…" and here he would hold up the broken sword suspended by the thong about his neck, "how the sword of death has been conquered by the cross of love. Behold and know that if I can be saved, then how much easier must it be for any of you to enter into the kingdom of God."

Though the message was powerful, it fell on deaf ears. Each time Cestus began to speak, people turned their backs and went quickly on their way. This stranger was not only an outsider but the most terrible of sinners as well. The one named Jarel had no right to introduce him among honest and upright men.

Finally, dejected and weary, the two turned their steps back toward Gedar. On the way they stopped near Mount Ebal, in Samaria, where Cestus tried once again to deliver his message.

"Rejoice!" he began. "Rejoice and accept the great gift that has been offered. For Jesus came to redeem humanity. He came bearing the gift of eternal life for us all."

"The Messiah was promised for the people of Israel and Israel alone!" someone shouted out.

"Jesus came with life for all," Cestus replied. "Jew and Gentile alike."

A murmur of protest arose at these words, and someone shouted out that next the speaker would declare that this Jesus loved even the Romans.

"And that we should all do likewise," a second man added derisively.

In the wake of the derisive laughter that followed, Cestus shocked his listeners by agreeing.

"Yes," he answered, swallowing hard against the words, for as long as he drew breath he would never forget what the Romans had done to Rachel. And yet, the message was clear. "In the sight of God, all men are brothers. Jew and Gentile, even the Romans."

At this a man spoke up and, with angry jabs of his finger, pointed out that the one who stood before them was not a prophet or a priest but a notorious slayer of men.

Cestus tried to raise his voice above the uproar to admit that this was in part true, that the fact of his past was central to his message. But the same man was yelling "Murderer!" at the top of his lungs, and others joined in with shouts of "Liar!" and "Blasphemer!" And amid the rising clamor, there came a demand that the imposters be stoned.

In a matter of seconds, the crowd was transformed into a pack of frenzied animals howling for blood. A stone flew from their midst and landed at Cestus' feet, then a larger one struck his shoulder, and yet another even larger rock struck Jarel squarely in the chest.

For one flashing instant, Cestus's eyes began to glaze over with the familiar red haze of fury. Clenching his fists and teeth, he struggled against it (seeing in his mind's eye the beast whirling before him, roaring to be released again), and when it seemed the power of the beast might overcome him, he instinctively called upon the name of Jesus, saying it aloud without thinking. And as he did so, the moment passed away.

Several men grabbed hold of Jarel and began to drag him away, having decided he was an easier prey than his much stronger looking companion. Cestus shouted for them to stop and began plowing his way through the men as though they were children. Startled by such a display of physical power, the men loosened their grip and stepped back.

Cestus pulled Jarel to his feet, then turned and opened his arms in a gesture of peace. "This man has done no harm to you, nor to anyone else," he declared. "If it is blood you must have, then have it from me. But spare this innocent man."

Not a single mouth opened in answer to his words. Men who were moments before bent on casting stones began to shuffle about uncertainly, exchanging furtive, sideways glances. Then the stoning committee hurriedly disbanded.

Shaking the dust of that place from their sandals, Cestus and Jarel once again turned their steps toward Gedar. Not until they were an hour's distance away did they stop to rest.

"I've been thinking," Cestus said to his weary companion. "My message was to go forth and bear witness to all people. Not just those in a chosen land, but all humanity. So why not carry the message to others like myself? To people counted as outsiders, as barbarians. What was it Jesus said to the disciples? I will make you fishers of men? Perhaps we have been fishing in the wrong pond." He paused, then said, "But it may be even more dangerous, so I'll understand if you don't want to go along."

Jarel waited a few moments, and then smiled. "You don't think I'm going to let you have all the fun by yourself, do you?"

XXXV

Sharra took considerable pleasure in the comforts and privileges her new station afforded her. There were fine quarters in which to live, an abundance of food and drink, and gowns and jewelry such as her eyes had never seen and her mind had not imagined. Moreover, servants looked after her needs so that her days were empty of labor. If the price of all this was not exactly to her liking, she consoled herself with the reminder that she had made far worse bargains in the past. Besides, she was growing ever more secure in her power over the Roman with three names, was becoming in ways more the master than the slave, more the possessor than the one possessed.

Yet there was that ceaseless torment, that festering obsession that would not give her rest.

Thus, when she received a startling bit of information from a secret and well-rewarded informant, she began to conceive her plans of revenge all over again.

She waited until Marcellus Servianus had eaten and drunk his fill at the evening meal before curling up beside him. "You know," she purred, "that I will be forever grateful for your kindness and generosity, not to mention your, uh, most intimate attentions. So I have made it my duty to be your eyes and ears, for one such as powerful as you will always have enemies waiting to take that power."

Marcellus Servianus looked at her with raised eyebrows. "I had no idea that you were so concerned, my dear. Tell me, have your eyes and ears discovered anything I should be aware of?"

"I believe so, my lord. I have heard rumors of a religious zealot wandering about the wilderness of Judea preaching the word of a crucified Jew named Jesus, who is said to have risen from the dead. It is further said that this Jesus had claimed to be the son of a god, and that he was expected to return in the near future to establish the kingdom of his father. And this newest zealot was certain to be an officer of power in the army of this kingdom."

"Ah…well, I appreciate your concern, but it seems that religious fanatics are a part of the Judean landscape. A new one pops up every other month and soon enough disappears. If this latest troublemaker chooses to go tramping about the wilderness, so much the better. He'll do little harm in such out-of-the way places."

"No doubt what you say is true, my lord, but there is more," Sharra persisted. "This particular zealot has recently returned to Palestine and is staying in the village of Gedar, in Galilee."

"The significance of all this escapes me," Marcellus Servianus said, stifling a yawn.

"I have learned," Sharra went on, watching his face closely, "that this man is none other than Cestus."

This last statement was so preposterous that Marcellus Servianus laughed out loud.

"He confirms it by his own mouth," Sharra went on. "He admits that he was a fighter in the arena, and afterward the leader of a warrior clan. But he claims to have had a vision. To have seen the crucified Jew alive and in the flesh. And he says that this Jesus told him to forsake the sword and go about proclaiming something called the power of the cross."

Marcellus Servianus stared at her in open-mouthed amazement. All this time she had kept it alive! All this time! Would she never give it up? The answer to that was apparent. But what after, when her revenge had at last been accomplished? What then? Had she merely been using him until such time, even more than he had been using her? The answer to this question was something he did not want to consider.

"What is this power of the cross?" he asked.

"The followers of this Jesus claim that he was the son of God," Sharra said. "They believe in only one god," she added, trying to explain something she did not herself understand except as it had been loosely interpreted to her. "They claim he let himself be crucified in order to prove his powers. To prove that he could come back from the dead."

Marcellus Servianus waved his hand for her to stop, then sat silently for some time, trying to piece things together. There was no reason to doubt that Cestus was somewhere in Asia Minor, but to accept the story that he had seen a vision and so converted from warrior to priest was straining the limits of belief. Yet, what Sharra reported could somehow turn out to be true (and here Marcellus reminded himself that when it came to Cestus anything even remotely possible should not be dismissed). Moreover, his experience with the people of that region had shown them to be unreasonable beyond compare, and as such they were likely to follow after anyone—even a man like Cestus.

Conjuring up a smile, he turned to Sharra. "My dear," he said, "are you certain of all this, or are you perhaps allowing your passion for vengeance to taint your reason?"

"I am certain, my lord," she said, saying the words with such certitude that any doubt he harbored was dispelled.

"And you think that I should dispatch troops to find Cestus?"

"It would seem a wise thing to do," Sharra answered, adopting the tone of a servant seeking only to be of use to her master. "Not only would such action blot out an enemy of Rome, but it would also serve you well to personally stem this uprising before it gets out of hand. Surely it would help you return to Rome in glory."

"Yes," Marcellus Servianus agreed. "So it would serve me well. And you also, of course…" That night Marcellus Servianus lay awake well after his normal hour of sleep, sorting things out in his mind. Sharra had given him information about Cestus before and had been essentially correct. So he would take this opportunity she had handed him to make an end of Cestus. Once this was accomplished, he would have the answer to an important question. Moreover, as Sharra had suggested, by preventing a potentially bloody revolt (for so this report would indicate), he would speed his triumphant return home.

Smiling to himself, he envisioned Sharra's reaction when she beheld the matchless splendor of Rome, for he had decided to take her back with him. All doubts would then be erased, all lingering thoughts of Cestus purged from her mind.

Yes, he concluded, beginning at last to close his eyes in rest. All doubts would then vanish. He would answer the question for himself, by himself…and in so doing exchange this miserable little kingdom for one far grander.

XXXVI

The two itinerant disciples crept carefully up a steep, thickly wooded incline, the smell of smoke and the sound of voices growing louder with every measured step. They stopped short of the crest and crawled the last few feet.

"I thought the places we've been to the last few weeks were rough," Jarel whispered, peering over the ledge, "but this looks like the worst I've seen yet."

Cestus surveyed what he could see of the ramshackle huts and pens below. Here and there he caught sight of a thick-bearded, hard-faced man, a bony, straggly haired woman, a lean-ribbed dog too lazy to bark.

"So far we haven't opened a single ear to the Word. My feet are blistered, my legs are tired, and my back hurts—but still I confess that I'm thankful."

Cestus looked over with a raised eyebrow, waiting.

"Thankful that my skinned hide is not being worn as a coat by one of these unwashed barbarians. Perhaps we should pass this place by. Go to my house in Gedar, eat, rest, and give thanks that we are still drawing breath."

"Some places look worse than others, some better." Cestus replied, getting to his feet. "I don't think it's up to us to choose in advance."

"Now you're beginning to sound like Zebediah," Jarel muttered, following Cestus down the sloping hillside.

As the inhabitants of the settlement caught sight of the approaching strangers, they stopped what they were doing to study the intruders with wary and unsmiling eyes.

"I really don't think it's wise to pause here," Jarel protested, lagging back a few paces.

Before Cestus could reply, a shrill cry pierced the tense stillness.

At the center of the settlement was a rough wooden enclosure in the form of a circle. Inside the circle several wild horses were milling around, snorting and rearing up to paw at the air with powerful hooves. A number of the men of the clan were gathered just outside the enclosure, apparently gathering up the nerve to enter and try their hand at taming the unbroken beasts, when suddenly a youth scarcely more than a boy climbed over the fence, let out his version of a war cry, and vaulted atop the back of a stallion.

The frightened and enraged animal whirled and kicked and bucked, but for a time the determined youth held on, whooping in triumph. Then, quite as suddenly as he had mounted the horse, the boy was thrown off. He struck the ground heavily and lay there unmoving as the beast reared and snorted and hammered its hooves into the earth.

The loosened fury of the stallion goaded the other horses into a frenzy, and they began to storm about the enclosure, threatening to break free. The attention of the entire compound was so riveted on that single spot that no one noticed Cestus until he was inside the barricade. Then all eyes were drawn to him in astonishment.

"Whoa, now..." he called in a low steady voice. "Whoa, now...Nobody's going to hurt you, boy." He approached the raging stallion with carefully measured steps, his voice trailing off to a whisper, and reached out and touched it. Placing his hands on the animal's neck, he moved with it, patting and stroking and soothing. And gradually it ceased to struggle.

When the stallion calmed down, Cestus turned his attention to the others. And in a short while he had them all under control. Only then did he turn to Jarel.

"Come and look after the boy," he said. "I will keep the horses calm."

Jarel entered very, very carefully. Kneeling over the youth, he saw that he was not dead, possibly not even badly injured. Evidently he had been knocked unconscious by the fall and by some miracle had escaped the horse's hoofs.

"He is alive," Jarel said, and with those words the boy opened his eyes as if returning from the dead.

That evening a feast was held to honor the two strangers who possessed such great power that they could tame wild horses with their bare hands—and bring the dead back to life. Perhaps, some of the villagers suggested, these two were gods, come down from the hidden hills.

Seizing the opening, Cestus replied that they were not gods at all, but rather were sent by the one true God. Then he spoke his message, and when he finished, he discovered a most amazing thing: The legend of Jesus, the son of God, had not penetrated to this remote place, but that of Cestus, the gladiator and warrior chieftain, had.

When the people began to question him about his metamorphosis, he told them how an evil spirit had once controlled his mind and body, and how Jesus had rid him of this spirit and given him a new life, with power beyond anything he had ever imagined. Not power of this world, but over it, so that he might have life everlasting.

His listeners were lost before such words. Some misinterpreted them to mean that Cestus had become immortal in a bodily sense, that he was, indeed, some sort of god, an invincible warrior who would live forever. But at least they listened. Of all those that Cestus and Jarel had thus far approached, only here in this most primitive of settlements did anyone listen.

The two apostles remained in the settlement of wild horses for several days, opening ears to the gospel and helping attend to the sick. And when they left, word of what they had said and done went out before them.

When they came upon the next settlement, one of the inhabitants walked up to Cestus and studied the hilt of the sword hanging about his neck.

"Cestus!" he pronounced. "Cestus!" he said again, turning to the others of his clan. And the single word went from mouth to mouth until it became a continuous chant, the broken syllables rising and falling in unison.

"Ces-tus!...Ces-tus!...Ces-tus!"

XXXVII

Before winter could trap them in the highlands, Cestus and Jarel returned to Besara. But the memories were sad there, and the village filled with ghosts. Long before the advent of spring they made plans to go again to spread the word.

The day before their departure, Cestus was checking on the roof when he heard the familiar cadence of marching feet, quick but measured and unhurried. His first thought was that he had not had nearly enough time to do his work. As they came into sight, he climbed down to face them.

The centurion in charge of the detachment had not only been given a detailed description of the one he was to take into custody, he had looked upon him firsthand in the arena. Now he studied the man before him.

"You are Cestus," he declared, and despite the sword in his hand and the armed troops at his side, he took an involuntary half step backward.

"My birth name is Steppan," came the reply, not in an argumentative fashion but quietly, as if the speaker simply wished to set the record straight.

The Roman pointed his sword at Cestus's chin. "I saw you in the arena," he said. "I know what I saw then, and I know what I see now. You are Cestus."

At that moment Jarel came hurrying up, demanding to know what was going on.

The centurion made a quick motion with his free hand, and two of his men grabbed Jarel and forced him to his knees. "You must be the one called Jarel," the centurion observed.

"I am," Jarel replied.

A slight smile creased the centurion's face. "At least you do not lie. Still, you must learn what it is to interfere with the power of Rome."

"Wait!" Cestus said. "It is true that I was once known by the name of Cestus. If it is him you search for, him you have found, but only in body."

"The body will be quite enough," the centurion smirked. He gave a sharp command, and several soldiers approached Cestus and bound his hands behind his back. When this was accomplished, the centurion inspected his prisoner more closely.

"So…this is the famed Cestus," he taunted. "The scourge of the arena. Well, come then, Cestus. You have a long walk ahead of you."

Two of the soldiers grabbed hold of Cestus and began propelling him along.

"No!" Jarel shouted, "Let him go!" He struggled to rise, but his efforts were futile; he was shoved back down and his face pressed into the dirt.

The centurion halted and looked over at Jarel once more. Slowly, almost lazily, he raised his right hand, then, without so much as a single word, brought it down in a swift and unmistakable gesture.

Before he could release the cry of horror welling up in his throat, Cestus heard behind him the sickening sound of sword striking flesh—but strangely muted, as if the blade was dull or had struck a block of wood. Wondering in that rushing moment of insanity that there had been no outcry of pain or dying, he twisted about (his movement heavy and slow, as if the air about him had turned to water), saw the blade go sweeping down a second time, and watched—unable to lift a hand or loosen his voice or even look away—as the head of the faithful Jarel tumbled onto the gray dust of the road.

Cestus was taken to Caesarea, where he was cast into a tiny cell deep beneath the great judgment hall. He had been in that damp subterranean vault scarcely an hour when he heard the steady approach of footsteps, dimly at first, then nearer and louder. And as he braced himself to face the unknown, a disjointed torrent of images swirled swift and unbidden before his mind's eye…

visions of a childhood forever lost in the smoke-filled darkness of that dreadful morning…

of the way the sand of the arena glared with such terrible brightness in the sun, burning your eyes when you emerged from the cramped darkness of the house of waiting…

of swirling dust that choked the sky, and the noise of trampling horses…

of dying men and screaming women, of pain and broken bodies and the soul-numbing madness of it all…

and just before the footsteps rounded the final corner of the unseen hall, he thought of a deep, clear night filled with the mystery of stars…

of a voice that called from somewhere beyond, yet sounded from within...
of two hands bearing gifts of wounds that pierced the hearts of men...

When the footsteps halted before the door of his cell, he forced himself to look up with the disciplined resolve of no-thought. But when he saw through the open doors of iron the one who had been escorted there, his mouth dropped open in shock.

Sharra!

The idea that she should be standing there was so incredible, so utterly inconceivable, that for a moment he thought it must be another vision. The bite of the irons at his ankles as he rose quickly to his feet let him know that he was, indeed, awake.

"So...it is you, Cestus," she breathed, her words trembling and uncertain, almost as if she found it all as difficult to accept as did the one she addressed. "At last, it is you..."

For several moments her eyes fastened on his, then tears blurred her vision and she turned and hurried away.

After Sharra and her escort of soldiers had departed, the jailer, a grizzled veteran with several missing teeth, came to the tiny cell. He opened the door and shoved in a cup of water, then lingered in the doorway, bursting with curiosity about the connection between such a striking-looking woman and the new prisoner.

"I've never seen a beauty such as that one down here," the jailer muttered, his tongue thick with lust. "What a piece she'd be, eh?" the jailer went on, rubbing his crotch and leering, recalling the woman's swaying hips as she had mounted the steps leading from the dungeon.

When the jailer got no response, not even a nod or an upward glance, he slammed and locked the door, then peered inside and tried once more. "How would you like to be locked up with her?" he smirked, briefly imagining her there, inside the cell, chained and helpless.

"I once was," came the reply, leaving the jailer even more perplexed than before.

It was not long before other visitors, members of the Legion quartered at Caesarea, began to wind their way down to the dungeon, for word quickly spread that the famous gladiator Cestus was locked away there. In the beginning, they merely approached the cell and stared, content to say that they had come and seen. Soon enough, however, because they were mostly young and bored, some of them began to harass the prisoner, mocking and jeering and taunting in an effort to dilute some of their misery by casting it upon another. And, as was bound to happen, one of them came seeking to build a reputation.

A large young man, thick of bone and muscle and skull, a brawler of considerable repute, approached the jailer and tried to convince him to turn the prisoner loose in order to stage a fight.

"We'll have our own private arena!" he thundered. "Clear out the holding cell and lock me inside with this Cestus!"

Because such an act would cost him more than just his job, the jailer refused, but the would-be challenger—who was accompanied by a retinue of admirers—was in no mood to be denied. "You can say he was killed trying to escape," he went on. "You can say anything you like, only let me fight him!"

The jailer wavered briefly before the ominous physical presence of his petitioner—that and the temptation to actually see such a match, for if the prisoner was, indeed, the legendary Cestus, then such an opportunity would come but once in a lifetime—but caught himself and held fast.

"You can make a whole year's wages betting on me to win!" the young hot head offered, but the jailer only looked away.

The continued denial so infuriated the self-styled gladiator that he went storming against the door of the cell that held the one he was raging to confront, pounding on the bars with such force that the entire hallway reverberated with the sound of his blows.

"Tell this old woman of a jailer to let us fight!" he bellowed to Cestus. But there was no response, not even a meeting of the eyes. "Look at me when I speak! Look at me! Do you fear the death I hold in these hands?" He held up his fists for display, then hammered at the iron bars a few more times before turning to his comrades with a sneer, satisfied that while he would not fight that day, he had at least proven his courage.

"No, I do not fear you."

The words were spoken so softly, so calmly, that they echoed with unnatural loudness in the wake of the mindless fury that had gone before.

The young soldier pivoted about and saw that the prisoner had risen and was standing by the door to his cell. "Then, you will fight?" he said, suddenly not quite so sure of himself.

From beneath a shroud of ashes, the shadow of the beast stirred yet again. Fight! it exhorted. Show this snarling dog the power of the hand of Cestus! Cestus hesitated before the temptation, and then answered it one final time.

"If you had come before me like this in the old days, I would have killed you," he said, pronouncing the words with no hint of boasting but as a simple matter of fact. "And in so doing, I would have been the one who lost. Now, even if I were loosened from these chains, I would not fight you, unless it was to save someone other than myself."

For several moments Cestus held the gaze of the soldier, trying to penetrate the invisible barrier that separated them more surely than any wall of stone or door with bars of steel, then the other man broke away.

"He's crazy!" the soldier declared to his comrades. "A madman. He's probably not Cestus at all!" Punching the empty air with clenched fists, he moved quickly away before the madman could change his mind.

When the hallway was empty again, the jailer went over and peered into the cell. The prisoner was on his knees, facing the far wall. His head was bowed, his arms outstretched, his hands raised up and open to something the jailer could not see.

XXXVIII

Marcellus Servianus Portius sank down into the warm water of his bath, trying not to contemplate the day that lay before him. The tub had been constructed to his precise specifications, and it had become one of his most prized possessions. Within its spacious confines he would slip down to his chin in warm, scented water and close his eyes. And all problems and confusions would temporarily be washed away.

This morning, however, his eyes would not stay closed for long. After only a short time in the bath, he abruptly stood, spilling water out over the sides and causing the Greek slave attendant to hurry to his side with a towel. The slave dried his master, and then assisted him to the rubbing table, where he anointed Marcellus's body with oil.

After the slave finished the massage and was dismissed, Marcellus Servianus surveyed his body with a small mirror, an act that proved to be a further irritation, for no matter how he turned the mirror, the body shown him was not that of a soldier or athlete, not lean or hard or marked with mementos of battle. Certainly it was not the physique of a gladiator. Rather it was the body of a wealthy and sedentary son of Rome—a body made soft by too much food and drink and too little effort.

Mumbling a curse, he let the mirror drop from his hand, but what it had reflected could not be so easily dismissed from his mind. Anxious thoughts about the shape of his own sacred body had first occurred to him when the slave boy named Steppan had been brought to Alba Longa some years before, but had not fully resurfaced until he had allowed himself to reflect on the depth of Sharra's passion for revenge. For when such examination revealed that her burning zeal to punish Cestus was nothing more than the reverse side of a coin of conflicting emotions, his towering but hollow vanity swiftly began to crumble.

So when Cestus was at last brought within his power, Marcellus Servianus could not summon the will to go and confront him, not even through locked bars of iron. When Sharra pressed him on this point, he told her that insomuch as she had already made positive identification there was no need for him to lower himself or his office by descending the steps to the dungeon. In due time, the prisoner would be brought forth.

Now, with the hour swiftly approaching when that prisoner would stand before him for judgment, a strange sense of anxiety darkened the moment. Only when he was in sight of the reassuring size and splendor of the great judgment hall was he able to leave a portion of his misgivings behind. It did, after all, promise to be a day of glorious triumph. A day in which he would disburden his mind of the specter of Cestus, grant Sharra her long-awaited vengeance, and perhaps even please his father. Yes, he assured himself, lengthening his stride, a day of triumph indeed.

Cestus paced slowly about the cell as he said his morning prayers. The first thing upon awakening, he would recite the prayer that Jesus had taught his disciples. Then he would ask the Lord Jesus to live within him that day, to grant the peace and love and joy of his presence. Next he would ask God the Father to give aid and comfort to those he knew to be in need, and afterward he would pray for the souls that had departed the earth, always saving mention of Rachel for last, dwelling with her awhile in memory according to the circumstances in which he found himself.

There was something else he would have added this day, but he did not know if it was worthy to ask for such a thing. It troubled him that he was to be brought before a tribunal with his hair uncombed and tangled, his clothes dirty and torn, his body badly in need of a bath, not because of personal vanity but because this day he would stand to bear witness to the Word. Yet perhaps it was better this way, he thought; it would be a sign that the outward world did not much matter.

Still and all, he would have liked to have a comb, some water with which to wash, and a garment to wear that had not been held captive with him in the dank and musty confines of the dungeon.

The sound of footsteps interrupted his thoughts. He looked up to see the flickering approach of a torch-bent shadow, and in a few moments the gap-toothed face of the jailer appeared. The jailer unlocked the door and thrust in a breakfast of bread and water, then looked quickly about, reached into his pocket, and brought out a wooden spoon and a handful of dates and figs.

"Here," the jailer grunted, placing the spoon and the fruit on the wooden bowl alongside the bread.

Cestus's eyes fastened on the unexpected pieces of kindness, then met those of the jailer. "Thank you," he whispered.

The jailer gave a depreciatory wave of his hand. "It's nothing," he said. He did not move to re-lock the cell but remained standing where he was while Cestus gave thanks over the food. Then he spoke again.

"So, then, tell me: are you Cestus the gladiator or not?"

Outside, the morning had risen, but in this place beneath the surface of the earth torches served as sunlight. Cestus studied the play of unsubstantial light on the jailer's face for a moment, and then set his meager breakfast aside.

"Yes," he replied, "I am known as Cestus. I was a gladiator, and a slave. But I won my freedom from both slavery and the arena."

"I don't understand," the jailer said, shaking his head. "I just don't understand. I have heard much of you. You claimed fame in the arena, silver and fame. And women!" By the uneven light of the torch, the jailer's eyes glowed with imagined pleasures. "And then you rode at the head of a warrior clan, free to go wherever you pleased. I know firsthand that even the Legion heard your name with fear! But you threw it all away! And now, when these braying young asses who call themselves soldiers come to taunt you, you say nothing! And you do nothing! You just sit there and look down at the floor."

"These men do not bother me. I have nothing to fear from them."

"Ah...of course. You could easily defeat any of them."

"Perhaps, but that is not what I meant. I have no fear because I have been reborn."

"Reborn?" the jailer asked, puzzled anew. "How can a man be reborn?"

"Through the power of Jesus, the living son of God. Through him I was reborn in spirit."

"In spirit?" The jailer frowned.

"This life is not for the body, my friend," Cestus said softly, "but for the soul. The way of Cestus was death and darkness, while the way of our Lord Jesus leads to life everlasting."

"Life everlasting! The jailer hawked and spit upon the floor. "This putrefying life I have is not worth the living. Why should I want to suffer with it forever?"

Cestus moved closer to the jailer and looked deeply into his eyes. "You call your life a putrefying existence. Hear me when I tell you that at the time when most men would have thought me at the height of my powers, I walked in a nightmare, a living hell. Of all the things I had known in my life, the one true good thing was the love of a woman. When that was taken from me, my spirit sought only death. But Jesus rescued me and showed me the way. You see, God lives within us. Yes," he affirmed, noting the expected look of disbelief on the jailer's face. "God is with us at this very moment, here and now, in this underground pit. But so, too, is the force of evil, with all the torments of the flesh. So it is that I must choose, and you must choose: Will it be the way of the world, which ends in death, or the way of Jesus, which is life everlasting in the kingdom to come."

"The kingdom to come? What kingdom is that?"

"It is a hard thing for me to explain, but the kingdom to come is not of this earth. It is a kingdom not of the sword but of love."

"A kingdom of love? Hah! How long do you think such a kingdom would last before the wrath of the Romans?"

Cestus shook his head, trying here in this dark, damp cell to bring to his jailer's troubled soul a glimpse of the heart-piercing light that had shattered his sword. "The kingdom of the Romans, as with all earthly kingdoms, will soon pass away, my friend. Of all the things known to men, only love will last forever. Consider this: if there truly was love in the hearts of all men, then no one would fear another, for where there is love there can be no fear. And if there is no fear, then no one would harm another. There would be no strife, no wars, and no bloodshed. All of God's people would live as brothers and sisters in peace and harmony. They would be as one."

The jailer's brow was so tightly wrinkled with questioning that his pain was clearly visible. "How do you speak so surely of such things?" he asked.

Cestus reached out and put his hand on the jailer's shoulder, a movement that was so kindly and natural that the jailer did not even think to object. "Let me tell you of a most strange and wondrous thing," he said.

For some time after Cestus was finished, the jailer stood without speaking, his eyes turned inward, then he turned and shuffled wordlessly away.

With an inward sigh, for he feared he had failed to deliver his message, Cestus turned his attention to breakfast. Just as he finished, the jailer returned bearing a tray on which there was a pitcher of water, a cloth for washing, a comb fashioned of wood, a small mirror…and a robe that was worn and faded but clean.

"I thought you might have use of these things," the jailer said, all but a touch of the former gruffness gone from his voice. "But say not a word of this to anyone. I am not yet ready for the life everlasting you speak of."

When the jailer was gone, Cestus washed as best he could, combed through his hair and beard, and changed into the clean robe. Then he took the wooden comb and, taking care not to damage the instrument, painstakingly etched a single word on the wall, determined to leave an answer to the question that burned not only within the jailer but within all men.

XXXIX

By both purpose and design, the judgment hall at Caesarea was a most imposing structure, a vast chamber of marble and stone that could be described as either splendid or dreadful, depending on what business a person had there. Cestus was delivered to the hall in chains by four guards armed with swords and spears. He was brought in through a side door that led directly to the dais and prodded to a table, where the guards arranged themselves stiffly about him, very much aware they were on public display.

Squinting at the unaccustomed brightness of the world above ground, Cestus looked out over the hall. Before him row after row of benches were filled with people. He felt a momentary flush of embarrassment at being exhibited in chains, and in so ragged a condition, then caught himself. It was not an hour of humiliation, but of triumph and joy, for all these people—all these souls—had been delivered to him. Not he to them, to the Romans and those they controlled, but they to him, row after row of human fields in which to plant the seed of the Word.

Blocking out his surroundings, he closed his eyes in prayer, seeking guidance. He had only begun to pray when he heard a disruption in the tone of the assembly, a collective intake of breath followed by a rippling renewal of the babble of voices. Looking up, he saw Sharra being escorted to the first line of benches. Again Cestus bowed his head in prayer, trying to shut out the cacophony of sights and sounds swirling about him and the thundering crescendo of his heartbeat within. After a wait of several minutes, a knot of lawyers and scribes filed to a table opposite the one occupied by the guards and the man they guarded, and when they were settled, Marcellus Servianus made his entrance. Without so much as a glance at the prisoner, the prefect assumed his place on the dais and imperiously thrust out his open right hand.

An official scurried over and presented a scroll. Marcellus Servianus took it and pretended to read, but his eyes soon edged up over the top of the parchment. Yes, he thought, his pulse quickening as he studied the man in chains. Older, of course. Much larger than he had been as a youth. Changed in that way and others with the passage of time, but it was him. Without a doubt, it was him.

He rolled the scroll in upon itself and tapped it several times against the sweaty palm of his hand, then cleared his throat and began.

"By virtue of the fact that the prisoner before us stands accused of crimes committed against the Imperial Army of Rome, as well as various and sundry other offenses, I will conduct this tribunal myself." He nodded toward the table of lawyers and scribes, and one of them stood and began to read off the offenses with which Cestus was charged—a list that included murder, treason, and sedition.

When the recital was completed, Marcellus Servianus unrolled the scroll again. "You are the one named Steppan," he intoned, reading from the document. "Formerly a slave, first the property of Lucius Cornelius Portius, a citizen of Rome, Legate of the First Rank and esteemed member of the Senate, then of one Antonius Cappio of Capua for whom you fought in the arena and there received the name of Cestus." Here he paused and looked at the accused.

"I am he," came the reply.

"And, therefore, you remember me," Marcellus Servianus prodded.

"Yes, I remember you."

Marcellus Servianus could not suppress the pleasure of a smile. "Well, then, Steppan...or is it Cestus?" He glanced down at the scroll, and then looked up with raised eyebrows at the assembly before him. "This man has so many crimes charged against him that he requires two names to answer them all," he remarked, an aside that drew a responsive burst of laughter.

"Perhaps we should call you Steppan-Cestus," he went on, turning his attention back to the accused. "Yes, that should do. Well, then, Steppan-Cestus, you have heard the charges against you. As a matter of course, this tribunal has full verification of such charges. Witnesses, documents of evidence, and so forth. However, in an effort to spare us all a lengthy morning of testimony, I am willing to grant you the privilege of speaking now in your defense—if you have a defense to present. Bear in mind, however, that all who speak here are sworn to tell the truth on pain of death."

Cestus nodded.

"And further understand that here, this day, I am the sole and final arbiter in all matters before me."

Again Cestus nodded.

"Good. Speak, then. No doubt it will amuse this assembly to hear what words you might be able to muster."

Cestus shifted his gaze upward and gathered his breath, seeking guidance before he spoke. You have delivered them to me, he silently prayed. Now give me the words to do your will. Clasping his hands tightly before him so that he would not lean on the table for support, he began. "The acts of which I have been accused are hard words. Yet, which of them can I deny?"

A murmur of surprise ran through the assembly at this unexpected opening. Marcellus Servianus looked over sharply at the prisoner. The fool condemns himself, he thought, barely able to suppress yet another smile.

"Were I to offer a defense against such charges," Cestus went on, "I might plead that when I first confronted the Legions of Rome it was to rescue a woman pursued by their soldiers. And the second time it was to defend myself against an attack. But in truth did I not commit murder long before by slaying my fellow men in the arena? Then it was by official sanction, but it was murder nonetheless.

"And did I not commit treason as well? But my crimes were not against the kingdom of Rome, but rather against the kingdom of God. So any defense would be nothing more than an empty play on words. Thus I stand before you this day not to offer a defense, but rather a thanksgiving. For I have been delivered here in order that I might share with you the good news of salvation. Behold: Even as my worst sins have been forgiven through the sacrifice of our Lord Jesus, so does forgiveness and salvation await each and every one of you."

Now a murmur of another sort echoed about the chamber, and with it the smile that had begun to form of the lips of Marcellus Servianus turned swiftly downward. "Careful, slave!" he warned, leveling a threatening finger. "You misuse the right of speech I gave you!"

"I am a slave no longer, or else I would not have been granted this trial," Cestus replied.

"Nevertheless," Marcellus Servianus snapped, "guard your tongue lest you lose it! I gave you leave to offer a defense, not to bore us with meaningless prattle!"

Cestus gave a slight bow of his head. "There are but a few more words I would add, and then I am done."

"Speak and be done, then," Marcellus Servianus said, trying to quell a growing uneasiness that something was terribly amiss, that this person before him—whether by the name of Steppan or Cestus or whatever—was not, despite all appearances, the same one he had once owned through his father.

Cestus shifted about in his chains and looked in turn upon guards and officials and the throng of spectators huddled on benches. At last he brought his eyes to Sharra, and in them she saw none of the things she expected: neither hatred nor anger nor fear nor desire for vengeance of his own, but rather an urgent plea for her to listen.

Locked into his eyes, Sharra found herself wondering at something she did not even begin to understand. For though Cestus looked and sounded like the very same man whose tent she had once shared, he clearly was not. By some act of magic he had been transformed.

"I was born Steppan, a son of the forest," he began. "When I was but a youth, my village was raided and I was sold into slavery. Later I was sold again, this time into the arena. As a fighter there, a killer of men, I performed so well that I was given the name of the instrument of death I wore—the Cestus. At length I won my freedom, and for some time wandered through strange lands as the head of a warrior clan. Then a gift of love was granted me, in the form of a woman named Rachel. Even then my heart was not truly changed, for a demon lived within me, and I welcomed it and let it rule the man. Then it came to pass that my Rachel was taken away, slain by the hand of a Roman soldier."

He paused, drew in a long breath and held it, steadying his voice before he continued.

"When this terrible thing happened, I made ready to loosen the demon, for I sought the unending blood of vengeance. But then I was given the greatest gift of all. The demon, the beast that lived within, was slain, and I was shown the path to life everlasting."

A current of disapproval had been threading through the assembly, and now the people began to mutter openly among themselves. By his words the prisoner seemed truly demented. The authorities must have seized the wrong man. No matter what this one claimed, he neither spoke nor acted like a gladiator or a warrior chieftain. He seemed much more like one of those wandering ascetics. Something was plainly wrong here, but when the prefect made no objection, sitting instead in silence like another ornament of stone affixed to his chair, the spectators quieted down, and once more the words of Cestus went forth.

"Jesus, the son of God, who was crucified only to rise again from the tomb, appeared to me in person. He called me by my given name of Steppan and showed me the marks of the cross on his hands. And then he told me it was time for the beast to die in order that the man might live. And then, with nothing more than the power of his voice, he shattered my sword—the sword that no man alive could withstand."

Cestus looked over at Marcellus Servianus and addressed him directly. "Allow me to add only this, and then I am finished. My body is yours to do with as you please." Having so spoken, he turned back to the assembly and lifted up his chain-shackled hands in an attitude of blessing.

"Hear and rejoice and believe, for I bring you good news," he proclaimed. "God sent his son into the world to save mankind from sin. By the sacrifice of the blood our Lord Jesus shed on the cross, we have all been cleansed. And by his resurrection, Jesus gave proof that the power of God's love will endure forever.

"Behold: I was the most wretched of all sinners! The lowest of the low! And yet even my sins have been forgiven and the gift of eternal life bestowed upon me. Think, then, how much easier it will be for even the least among you to enter into the kingdom of God.

"Believe that Jesus came into the world for your salvation. Accept the gift of love that has been offered you. Accept and rejoice and be saved!"

With these words Cestus breathed a heavy sigh and leaned against the table. Did so much as even one of them hear? he wondered. Did even a single one of them receive the message into their hearts? Closing his eyes and ears to the clamor of voices about him, he prayed that he had not spoken in vain.

Marcellus Servianus waited for some time, savoring the moment, before he rose up from his throne and held his right hand aloft. When the hall was in total silence, he made his pronouncement.

"I have listened to the testimony of this man," he said, a harsh note of triumph ringing in his voice. "And by his own tongue he has condemned himself. Not only has he admitted to the several charges against him, but he has voluntarily added to the list. Therefore, this tribunal can do nothing other than find him guilty as charged. Thus be it known and recorded, that by the power and authority vested in me according to the decree of Tiberius Claudius Nero Caesar, Emperor of Rome, I hereby sentence the prisoner to death."

XXXX

"Lord," Cestus whispered aloud, "I am not worthy to ask for deliverance from what is about to happen, but give me strength and understanding so that I may pass this test for your greater glory."

His prayer was interrupted by the sound of a key in the lock to the cell door. He looked up to see the jailer enter with a jug of water and a bowl of grain, the food that was to be his last supper.

The jailer placed the jug and bowl before the prisoner, then, without bothering to look around to see that all was clear, took out a pouch with bits of roasted lamb and dried fruit and added it to the bowl of grain.

"Thank you," Cestus told him, focusing then on the other man and his act of charity and so forgetting at least a portion of himself.

The jailer shrugged, as if to say it was nothing, but did not move to go.

Cestus took a bite of lamb and washed it down with a sip of water, then stopped, waiting.

"Do you really believe those things you say?" the jailer blurted out.

"Yes," Cestus said. "I do."

"And what of the morning? Do you believe you will die? Or do you believe that your Jesus will come to save you?"

"Jesus has already come to save me, my friend. And so with the morning, my body will die, but my soul will have eternal life."

"But do you not fear the death of your body?"

"Yes," Cestus admitted. "I know fear. But in my heart I know that I have been redeemed from my sins. And so my fear passes, and in its place I am filled with great joy, for with the morning I will step from the floor of this dungeon to the gates of the kingdom of heaven."

The jailer moved deeper into the cramped cell. "Where might I find such joy?" he rasped, his voice hollow with despair.

"I am told there is a centurion named Cornelius who is a believer. Seek him and tell him you wish to receive the Word. When you have received the Word into your heart, you will know the path to such joy."

The jailer nodded. "This I will surely do," he declared. He shuffled to the door, then paused and turned about. "I can bring you a little wine," he offered, "so that this night might pass more easily."

"Thank you, my friend," Cestus said, "but I would face this night with a clear mind."

Alone again in his cell, Cestus continued his thoughts and his prayers, the two now so intermingled as to be almost one. How many times he had faced man's timeless foe in the arena or on the plains and mountains of battle he could not begin to say, and always there had been a fear so overwhelming that the man became lost and the beast burst forth unbidden. Then he had been considered fierce and brave above all others. But now, with no chance to escape from the invisible foe, he reached out for the true hand of strength—and that hand reached out in return.

The stones of his cell were growing cold when the opening of an outer door aroused him. Wondering how it could be that the hour had so quickly come, for he had not closed his eyes except in prayer, he struggled to his feet. But instead of the expected heavy cadence of marching boots, he heard a muted and solitary rustle of slippers. In a few moments, the door to his cell was opened... and Sharra entered unescorted.

"Cestus!" she cried, her eyes blurred by tears. "I caused all this!"

"No," he said moving closer to her. "You were only the instrument that brought me here. That much of the riddle I have solved. I must have hurt you deeply," he added, his voice touched with remorse.

Sharra let out a low moan and quickly turned away, biting her lips until her tongue tasted blood. How could he speak of having hurt her, when by her actions she had sentenced him to death? And how could it be that the face and body of Cestus existed as before, but the spirit had been so greatly changed? How, except that the words he spoke were true. Dabbing at her eyes with the corner of her shawl, she gathered the courage to face him. No doubt the jailer was straining to listen, but the ears of others did not matter now.

"I love you," she said. "From the very first, I loved you. Even through all the time of hating you, of crying for revenge, I still loved you."

"And I love you, Sharra," he said in return, saying it truthfully and without artifice of any kind, and though it was not the love she would have wished for, at the moment it was enough.

"Can you forgive me?" she whispered.

"There is nothing to forgive. A power far greater than me set us both on this path."

"But can you?"

"Yes, of course. Of course I forgive you, Sharra."

There was no stemming the flood then. She came into his arms, and he held her strongly and gently and tenderly, comforting her as best he could. When her sobbing at last subsided, he stepped back and sought the depth of her eyes.

"There is a centurion named Cornelius on duty in this city," he said. "Find him, Sharra, and tell him you wish to receive the Word. When you have received the Word, your tears of sadness will be washed away."

After Sharra departed, he sat down and leaned against the wall. Now that it was coming to an end, he reflected that it had all been so fleeting that it could have been a dream. And so beautiful, regardless of all the sadness and pain. So unutterably beautiful and mysterious and wondrous a dream from which he would soon awaken.

Closing his eyes, he saw again the great night sky of his childhood, ablaze with stars. He beheld it with speechless wonder, and in the midst of its infinite and unfathomable vastness, there appeared an opening, a cosmic window, as if the dwelling place of the eternal God was parted in welcome. Letting go of himself, he entered, and found Rachel waiting on the other side. Wrapped in a brilliant light that was at once too dazzling for the eye to behold yet as delicate and pure as the new day dawning, she was as radiant and beautiful as life itself. She smiled and beckoned, and the light went forth from her like a rainbow, wrapping the two lovers together.

When the jailer looked in on Cestus, he saw to his amazement that the prisoner was soundly sleeping. But what he could not see was the unspeakably pure light that filled the other man's soul, or the joyous pounding of his silent heart that was a drumbeat to summon the morning.

ABOUT THE AUTHOR

Arley Vest was born in St. Louis, Missouri, attended colleges and universities in Missouri and Louisiana, has lived in Missouri, Louisiana, Florida, California and the Gulf Coast of Mississippi, and currently resides near Atlanta, Georgia.

He is the founder and President of Lazarus Labs, a global non-prescription pharmaceutical firm. A member of good standing of the American College of Sports Medicine, he has owned medical weight loss clinics and fitness centers in Florida, Louisiana and Mississippi and hosted the television exercise show "The Body Shoppe".

In addition to *Cestus*, Arley has written a children's book, *The Land of No Day*, which has been produced as a play in schools in New York, Louisiana and Mississippi, has authored articles in national and regional magazines, and is currently at work on another novel.

More information can be found at www.arleyvest.com.
Contact: PO Box 469, Cassville, Georgia 30123

Made in the USA
Charleston, SC
08 February 2015